Canadian **Dani Collins** knew in high school that she wanted to write romance for a living. Twenty-five years later, after marrying her high school sweetheart, having two kids with him, working at several generic office jobs and submitting countless manuscripts, she got The Call. Her first Mills & Boon novel won the Reviewers' Choice Award for Best First in Series from *RT Book Reviews*. She now works in her own office, writing romance.

Also by Dani Collins

What the Greek's Wife Needs
Her Impossible Baby Bombshell
One Snowbound New Year's Night
Cinderella for the Miami Playboy

Signed, Sealed...Seduced

Ways to Ruin a Royal Reputation

The Secret Sisters

Married for One Reason Only
Manhattan's Most Scandalous Reunion

Discover more at millsandboon.co.uk.

INNOCENT IN HER ENEMY'S BED

DANI COLLINS

MILLS & BOON

First published in Great Britain 2022
by Mills & Boon, an imprint of HarperCollins*Publishers* Ltd,
1 London Bridge Street, London, SE1 9GF

www.harpercollins.co.uk

HarperCollins*Publishers*
1st Floor, Watermarque Building,
Ringsend Road, Dublin 4, Ireland

Large Print edition 2022

Innocent in Her Enemy's Bed © 2022 Dani Collins

ISBN: 978-0-263-29575-7

11/22

In loving memory of my mother, Sharon,
who taught me to love reading and
left romance novels on the coffee table
and showed me what a loving relationship
looks like with her fifty-five-year marriage
to my dad.

We all miss you, Mom.

CHAPTER ONE

THIS MUST BE what it would feel like walking to the gallows, Ilona Callas's imagination whispered as she passed through the security gauntlet in the lobby of the Vasilou Tower.

Her skin was clammy and her stomach was filled with lead. Her heart raced and her breathing was so shallow and rapid, she grew lightheaded. Her nostrils burned with the scent of danger. *Flee!*

Perhaps it was the glass elevator. The guard showed her into it and pushed the button, but left her to rise alone. She averted her gaze from the way the plants and people abruptly shrank beneath her and grasped the rail for balance.

She didn't care for heights, not since her older half brother Midas had dragged her to the edge of a cliff and terrorized her with threats of throwing her off. *A joke*, her stepmother had insisted. *Boys will be boys.*

Deep down, Ilona suspected the reason she

was here was because Midas was at it again. He was so funny with his destructive pranks, he ought to have his own comedy special on the streaming networks.

The Parthenon came into view then even that behemoth shrank as she continued to rise. Buildings this tall were a rarity in Athens. Most kept to twelve floors or less, ensuring the Parthenon was always in view. The fact the owner of this tower had been allowed to double that height told her he did not confine himself to the rules that governed others.

Much like Midas.

The knives in her stomach turned.

The door pinged and opened. Ilona entered a top floor reception area of stunning design. The marble tiles were arranged so the veins created a river effect, guiding her through a gallery of modern art to a desk stationed before a glass wall etched with a map of the globe.

A woman sat behind the desk, but a scrupulously groomed young man stood by to greet Ilona.

"Kyría Callas. *Kaliméra.* I'm Androu. Kýrie Vasilou will be with you shortly. May I ask you to wait here?" Androu led her to a door adjacent to the reception area, one that opened into a small, stuffy glass-fronted room. It held a round table and four chairs that were a chic, modern design made from polished wood. He didn't offer coffee or water before he left her.

The lack of respect was obvious. This room was a prison where she had no privacy. The lighting was artificial, the music not piped in. The only sound was the loud tick of the clock. Ilona didn't bother trying her phone. The service would be poor; she was sure. This room was deliberately uncomfortable so meetings here would be kept short.

It was not the place to leave a peer.

If Leander Vasilou thought she would depart in a huff of indignation, however, he was deeply mistaken. Ilona had been insulted, attacked and disregarded her whole life. Rather than taking offense, she was grateful for the time to sit quietly and escape the coming confrontation with more pleasant thoughts.

She admired that marble floor and wondered how she might obtain the name of the mason so she could plagiarize the effect in her flat. Or, as she often fantasized, perhaps she would sell her flat and move to the island of her mother's birth. She loved her work, but today was a perfect example of why it was also draining. It would be far less stressful to work in a café the way her mother had. On Paxos, she would have a view of actual water. She could feed the stray cats and try her hand at pottery. That had always fascinated her. So tactile and magical to create shapes from silt. She would have to look up whether there were appropriate clay deposits—

"Kyría Callas?" Androu was back. "Kýrie Vasilou will see you now."

A glance at the clock revealed she had been waiting thirty-three minutes.

Since the young man held the door with an air of expectation, she rose.

"Thank you," she said, but the blanket of dread returned to her shoulders, heavy and cold.

She followed him down a blessedly air-conditioned corridor, through a far more comfortable waiting area, one that provided a small banquet of refreshments and a view of the city.

He waved her into a massive office.

Here, the marble veins in the floor created a mountain effect. On one side, there were a sofa and chairs with a television mounted above a wine cooler set in a cabinet of glasses and bottles of spirits. The other side held a meeting table with six ergonomic chairs, a projector and a blank whiteboard.

In front of her, at the pinnacle of the mountain, natural light poured through a wall of glass, backlighting the occupant of the office, Leander Vasilou.

He sat at a desk made from a curved slab of polished mahogany set atop drawers arranged in a slant. The whole thing looked offset, but dynamic and ultramodern. He wore an earpiece and was speaking in French, booking a tennis match with someone.

The doors closed behind her, but his conversation only lapsed into whether a certain piste at a Swiss ski resort had been attempted, then the merits of protein shakes over whole foods after working out.

He didn't look at her once.

Ilona hadn't been invited to sit so she didn't. She waited with the patience she had gathered around her through a lifetime of being least and last and deeply unwanted. It usually served her well, cushioning her against most of life's spears and arrows.

Not today.

She knew he was aware of her, knew he was deliberately trying to get under her skin. To her chagrin, it was working. She wanted to put it down to the attack this stranger was waging on her. Many would label it "just business," but it was deeply personal to her. It was *her* business he was attacking.

That wasn't what was piercing her bubble of detachment, though. It was him.

She had seen photos of Leander Vasilou, but she hadn't expected his suit-model looks to be so mesmerizing in real life. His eyelids sat heavy and bored over gray irises. A scruff of beard accentuated the height of his cheek-bones and the hollows of his cheeks. That same scruff might be hiding a cleft in his squared off chin. It certainly framed a mouth that gave her a small thrill when his teeth briefly caught at the inner flesh of his bottom lip.

"Oh, yes, I remember her very well," he said, voice dipping into smoky amusement rife with sensual memory.

That tone had the strangest effect on her,

turning the greasiness of dread in her belly to warm butter laced with honey.

A flush of heat rose from that same place, radiating into her breasts and turning to an embarrassed heat as she realized she was reacting in a very sexual way to that timbre in his voice.

She *never* reacted to men. Or women. Not to anyone. Not like this. She dated when an escort was expected—like a gala or holiday party—but she rarely allowed more than a kiss at the end because that was when her interest always dried up.

Oddly, this man, whom she was predisposed to fear and dislike, was making her wonder how his lips would feel against her own. How would they feel in the crook of her neck? His wide hands became a source of fascination as he briefly squeezed the back of his neck and laughed, causing the fabric of his shirt to strain across his well-built shoulders and thick biceps.

She had never once in her life felt her breath leave her because the beauty of a man appealed so strongly. Or experienced a compulsion to unbutton a man's shirt and nuzzle the hair on his chest because a few fine hairs at his collar caught her attention, but she was envisioning doing that to him and was appalled with herself.

She swallowed, discovering her throat was hot and tight. Her cheeks were beginning to sting as her blush arrived from her chest and swept upward.

She averted her gaze to a sculpture that could have been steel flames. She thought about the time Midas had thrown her doll into the fire at the Pagonis chalet in Switzerland. It had been the last thing her mother had given her.

That painful memory helped her remember why she was here. At nine, she hadn't had the courage to pluck her doll out of the fire and save it. She wouldn't be so cowardly today.

She firmed her feet to the floor and drew a long subtle breath of patience.

Leander Vasilou finally ended his call. He dropped his earpiece onto his desk and looked at her with a distinct lack of interest.

"Kyría Pagonis. You wanted to see me." He didn't rise, didn't offer his hand to shake.

She didn't even glance at either of the chairs she stood between.

"Callas," she corrected with a polite smile. "My mother wasn't married to my father so

I use her name." Ilona always corrected that. It was a whole thing with Odessa, her stepmother. "But given you're attempting to take over my company, I expect you already know my name."

"I *am* taking over your company," he assured her. "Ilona."

His facetious tone was dangerously close to that other, intimate timbre he had used a moment ago. It had the same effect of unfurling frond-like sensations deep in her belly.

She tried to ignore it, but her throat was constricting again.

"You have acquired forty percent of the shares in Callas Cosmetics. I own forty-five. Pagonis International owns the remaining fifteen, so I don't know how you—"

"Does it?" he cut in.

The sweet sensations in her stomach curdled. The text from her younger half brother Hercules appeared in her mind's eye.

You should be here. They're making decisions without you.

"I understand you've made an offer to buy those shares from Pagonis. May I assume you're prompted by product loyalty? Your skin is certainly flawless," she said.

There was a flash behind his sharp gaze, like the glint off a knife blade.

"You may assume that my intention is to take over Pagonis International. Acquiring their cash cow is the first step."

Ilona had been called many things, but never that. And Midas must know he was the real target. That's why he was throwing her company forward as a sacrifice. Big surprise.

She tightened her grip on her clutch, fighting to keep an impervious expression on her face.

"I've bettered your offer," she said with false calm. "If they sell, it will be to me. I'm here to offer for the forty percent you've already obtained. I'm prepared to pay above market value."

"I've upped the ante myself, promising ten percent over any offer you make. The sky is the limit. That was one of the Pagonis board members on that call." He flicked a finger toward his earpiece. "We're old friends and he owes me a favor. He's also greedy as hell. Pagonis will not be selling their shares to you."

The churn in her stomach grew into a tangle of thorny brambles.

"Why is it that you're targeting Pagonis?" she asked, lifting her brows in absent interest. "Cosmetics and biotechnology fall outside the Vasilou bailiwick, doesn't it?" His conglomerate took on large infrastructure projects like bridges and airports.

"I want to take back what's mine and destroy the rest," he said very casually, as though mentioning his errands for the day.

Her blood went cold as she began to see where Midas was dragging her. Here was the cliff, and its churning sea was in Leander's eyes, mercilessly crashing against sharp rocks.

"What, um, what exactly is yours?" she inquired, fighting to keep a level tone.

"The speech recognition technology that your brother 'developed' sixteen years ago." He only curled the fingers on one hand to indicate the air quotes, not even lifting the heel of his palm off the blotter on his desk. Contempt dripped off his tongue. "Most of the credit goes to my father, but I worked with him on it. Then Midas talked us into allowing him to assist us with taking it to market. That was the last we saw of him or any profit we should have earned."

Of course, Midas had stolen that technology. She kicked herself for not seeing it long before now, but she had still been at boarding school when he had been impressing their father with his business acumen. Then she had focused on building her own enterprise, distancing herself as much as possible from Midas and the corporate headquarters, not wanting to work at Pagonis International because she would have to work directly under Midas.

"That doesn't explain why you're coming after my company, rather than some of the subsidiaries that Midas controls," she said.

"I entered the door that was open. Your shares aren't as expensive or well-protected against speculative trading. Which doesn't make sense to me when your company has been infusing the mother ship with much-needed cash for over a year."

It made sense if he knew her family, but she didn't let their greed and scorn of her value distract her in this moment.

"Your intention is to persuade the board to sell you its share in Callas Cosmetics and take it over from me? Then what do you plan to do with it?"

"Let it wither and die."

That pushed her onto her back foot. "Why?" she asked with anxious bafflement. "You just called it a cash cow."

"Because I want your family to know that I don't need it the way you do. I want it to *hurt*. I want you all to feel sickened at the mistake you made, living off the fruits of my father's labor, stealing the credit and driving him to ruin."

The gravel rolling in her middle stopped. It became heavy and nauseatingly hard, but at least it was a feeling she was used to. This was very familiar ground.

"Your takeover is motivated by vindictiveness," she acknowledged.

"Yes." No hesitation or apology.

Perhaps he was entitled to his antipathy, but *she* hadn't stolen from his father. There was no defusing hate, though. Ilona had learned that with Odessa. It didn't matter that Ilona was her father's mistake. Ilona had always borne the brunt of Odessa's resentment.

That seemed to be what Leander had in store for her. He would take the majority share in

Callas Cosmetics, then force her to watch as he ran it into the ground. That would crush her, given she had built it from a patch of dry skin on her cheek to a global enterprise.

A familiar despair at injustice floated around the edges of her periphery, but she mentally batted it away. Crying or fighting against the bullies of the world had never served her. The best she could do was soften the punch and get away as quickly as possible.

"I don't want innocent employees to lose their jobs." She made her decision with the swiftness of self-preservation and acted on it before second thoughts could creep in. "Our customers depend on the efficacy of our products, especially those with facial scars and burn injuries. It would be a shame to deny them something they need. I propose you buy my shares."

He snorted and his chair squeaked as he threw himself back in it. "I know what it looks like when a rat jumps ship, Ilona."

No fernlike tickle when he said her name this time. She was nothing but granite inside, hardened with resolve.

"I propose that you buy my shares for the amount my father gave me when he approved my business plan. That was one hundred thousand euros of start-up capital and a fifteen percent share. I don't know what I'll do next, but I'm happy to maintain those terms on any venture I pursue." A café, for instance. With dolmades served on hand-thrown crockery.

He was taken aback, not that he showed it, but he went very still and his eyes narrowed as he tried to discern what the catch might be.

She enlightened him. "In return I would insist you hire a qualified CEO and do everything in your power to keep Callas Cosmetics thriving."

"Your forty-five percent is worth ten million euros."

"Yes, I know." She offered a flat smile. "And I assure you that if you pursue the Pagonis shares just so you can destroy Callas, I will drive up the price until you pay thirty million for *fifteen* percent. Or you may have forty-five for one hundred thousand. My research tells me you're a shrewd negotiator. Well done."

"Your negotiation skills are terrible. What would you get out of that?"

Freedom.

"A clean conscience," she said. "I accept that I benefited from your father's work. It was unknowing, but I did. Losing ten million is a blow. Losing something I built with great pride and care would also cause me great distress. But having served me my just deserts, I assume you'll leave me alone in future." She hoped.

He steepled his fingers and swiveled his chair, head cocked as he reassessed her. "Are you trying to protect Midas by handing me the keys to your company? Did he send you here to make this little gesture to distract me from going after Pagonis International? It won't work. I won't give up."

She bit back a hysterical laugh. "I can see you're very determined." His ruthlessness was glowing like a neon sign. "The only people I'm trying to protect are the innocent ones."

Her employees from top level to floor-sweeper were a tight, dedicated team. There was already an ache behind her breastbone at knowing she wouldn't see them every day, but she was good at compartmentalizing. Showing this man how distraught she was wouldn't help her case. In fact, he would probably use it against her.

She stood tall and aloof as she waited for his next move.

His head fell back as he regarded her through the screen of his spiky lashes. "Are you angling to stay on as CEO?"

"No." She suppressed another choke of laughter. "My company is being used as a pawn between you and Midas. I refuse to become one myself. Take the spoils and fight your fight, but leave me out of it. Shall I have the paperwork drawn up?"

"Your eagerness to run is suspicious." His gaze flickered all over her, leaving little burn marks everywhere it touched.

She had made a mistake. She preferred to stay in the background, but she had caught his full attention and it was deeply disconcerting, both because his antagonism was plain and because she was reacting to him in such an inappropriate way. Some girlish part of her was squirming, worried her hair was out of place or there was a drip of coffee on her blouse.

"What if I asked you to stay on as CEO?" he questioned. "What if I made that my condition for accepting your offer?"

Her heart skipped then stretched with longing. She had built her company with more than pride and care. She had put her soul into it. She didn't care that her father had eventually decided Midas was the better businessman based on his stolen technology and named him president of Pagonis International. Ilona knew in her heart she outpaced Midas when it came to financial intelligence, marketing insight and management skills.

Much as it would kill her to walk away from what she had created, however, the idea of finally escaping the Pagonis tentacles was even more appealing. That 15 percent in Callas Cosmetics had kept her beholden to Midas after their father passed. If she gave up her company, however, she had no reason to continue associating with any of them.

She would finally be free.

Thanks to this man with the broad shoulders and glinting silver eyes and a sensual mouth that put shocking thoughts in her head.

"Tempted?" he chided in that infuriatingly seductive tone.

"No," she lied. Her skin was still prickling, wondering if he found her appealing which was so stupid. "The idea of partnering with a man who hates me and wants to use me to exact revenge against my family sounds like a marriage best not undertaken. I suggest—"

"Marriage," Leander cut in, sitting straight up with another screech of his chair. "Now *there's* an idea."

CHAPTER TWO

"WHAT?"

Ilona Callas's eyes widened as Leander shot to his feet and came around his desk toward her. In fact, there was a split second where he glimpsed genuine fear flare behind her startled gaze.

Then she blanked her expression and seemed to subtly rebalance her weight, but her knuckles turned white where she held her shiny black handbag. The tendons in her neck stood out with distress.

With a disconcerting swerve in his chest, Leander veered across the room to throw ice into glasses. He opened a bottle of sparkling water, glugging it over the cubes, using the action to steal a moment of reassessment.

Marriage to the illegitimate Pagonis daughter had already occurred to him as the ultimate means to his revenge, of course it had. For a decade and a half, he had mulled every possible path into their empire.

He had set aside approaching Ilona for several reasons, the primary one being that it would tip his hand. Making a stealth move on her company had put him in this first, fail-safe position of having a foot in the door. Morally, he had balked at romancing a woman under false pretenses, even one whose family he categorically despised.

Now that he had met her and she had brought it up, however, marriage returned as a possibility. That stark fear he had just witnessed was concerning, though. It had even briefly eclipsed his blinding desire to destroy the Pagonis family. Much as he wanted to make them pay, terrorizing a woman with sexual threats was not something he would ever do, under any circumstance.

Most especially if he was trying to talk her into marriage.

Is that what he wanted, though? Marriage? To *her*?

"I realize you didn't steal the tech yourself, but you've lived off those profits, Ilona. That's how your father was able to invest in your company. That's why I'm coming after you along with the rest. You don't get to be a Pagonis only when it works to your advantage."

There was such a loaded silence behind him, he glanced over his shoulder.

Her glower at his back quickly reconfigured into calm dignity. "I just offered to make good on that."

She had and he was still puzzling through that offer.

He set the fizzing glasses on the coffee table, nodding at her to join him as he took his customary armchair.

After the briefest of hesitations, she came to perch on the corner of the sofa farthest from him, ankles crossed, hands folded, demeanor one of polite interest.

Damn, but she was beautiful. He had noted that, too, in his many online research trips, but he was far more interested in whether a woman had an engaging personality or a unique perspective on life that challenged his own.

Still, he was red-blooded enough to react to Ilona's unadulterated sex appeal. She had a supermodel figure—tall and slender, but rounded in all the most alluring places. Her bone structure was delicate, but her depthless brown eyes were steady and unflinching. Her shiny black hair was clasped behind her neck. Her manicure and makeup were natural shades. Even her lipstick was a nude shade with only the barest hint of berry pink.

Somehow that was more tantalizing than garish red, drawing his gaze back to her wide, lush mouth again and again.

She wore simple gold jewelry—hoops in her ears, a chain with an ornate knot that sat in the hollow of her throat and a ring designed like ivy that twined toward the knuckle on her middle finger. Her clothing was a classic navy skirt suit with a pinstripe and a white shirt with its collar popped. Her shoes were a matching blue-black with red soles.

She wasn't flirting or throwing out lures, though. So he wasn't sure why he felt such a tremendous *pull*. It had accosted him the moment she had entered his office, quiet and graceful as a ballerina. Slithered, he had told himself of her near-silent entry. He wanted to view her as a viper, like Midas.

She was too sensual looking to be a cold-blooded reptile, though. He couldn't tell what she was beneath her understated, faultless demeanor.

Inexplicably, a hummingbird came to mind, one that appeared pretty and small when she was still, but with a heart that was beating a mile a minute. He didn't know that, but he sensed the way she remained alert, ready to dart away at the least startling movement.

She didn't touch her water, didn't fidget or press him to speak. She sat very quietly, exactly as his receptionist had reported she had behaved in the pressure cooker, the room in the reception area where he sequestered those he didn't really wish to see.

Rather than grow overheated and angry at his rudeness, or trying to maximize her time by making calls, Ilona had sat and waited.

Waiting was hard. Leander knew that because he had had to wait for his opportunity to take Midas down. The wheels were in motion but had yet to pick up momentum. Marriage to Ilona could provide the rocket fuel, but thinking about something like that and doing it were very different.

She was a Pagonis and not to be trusted.

On the other hand, she held a stake in the

company. Pagonis International was publicly traded, but the family owned a substantial interest. Their father had bequeathed his shares equally between his three children. His widow owned a similar amount and the family always voted together, maintaining control.

But what if Leander could disrupt that? At the very least, marrying into that family would allow him to reap some of the financial benefit that should have been his all along.

He nodded, warming even more to the idea of capturing this reluctant little pawn.

"You're not married," he noted. "Are you engaged? In a relationship?"

"I don't think it would be wise to offer you any more leverage than you currently possess," she said with a faint smile.

"Interesting that you think a relationship would be a weakness, not a strength."

"Goodness," she said with a glance at her naked wrist. "Did my therapy appointment overlap with my business meeting? I'll speak to my assistant. There's no reason you should feel compelled to do double duty."

He refused to like her, but he was a sucker for

sarcasm delivered on such a frosty platter. *May I assume you're prompted by product loyalty?*

He was still privately smirking over that cheeky remark.

"I find committed relationships to be a liability myself," he volunteered, presuming he would have unearthed any serious liaisons while he'd been researching her and her family. "I have no problem with monogamy, but demands on my time are very high. I don't like people in my space, expecting me to answer to them. I don't like being emotionally accessible. It's…*tedious*."

"Hmm." The noncommittal noise neither agreed nor disagreed.

Such a mysterious creature. He was reluctantly curious, wondering what it would take to get a real reaction out of her. Not a reflex like pain or fear. Laughter. *Passion.*

She must possess some of the latter. Callas Cosmetics was enormously successful in a crowded market. Her father's initial investment was well-documented, and the family name had definitely helped her along, but she hadn't relied on gimmicks or risky gambles or dirty plays that he could find. She had scaled strategically, always raising money through outside sources with sound proposals.

As someone who had grown his own business from next to nothing, Leander knew there had to be a deep emotional driver to propel a person into doing the hard work every day. His motivator was revenge. The way Ilona was prepared to sacrifice herself for her employees and customers suggested something less dark. It had to be passion.

He could definitely work with that.

"If we were to marry—" he began, then surprised himself with a fantasy of her long, slender legs squeezing his waist while he plumbed the depths of her sensuality, his mouth catching her cries of culmination.

A hot bolt of desire grounded itself behind his fly, causing the flesh there to twitch and thicken. He bit back a curse, nearly missing what she was saying.

"You have completely misconstrued my remark." She brushed at her knee. "I meant that taking a position under you in my own company sounds like an arrangement that is doomed to fail. It would be similar to a marriage where everyone says, 'It was obvious from the beginning that it wouldn't work out.' I don't like making obvious mistakes."

"Thank you for connecting those dots for me. I've moved to a new page where I am proposing—" Was he really going here? *Taking a position under you...*

Her words rang in his ears, but this wasn't about sex. It was about using her as a Trojan horse to get inside the family so he could deal Midas the lethal blow he deserved.

"I propose you allow me to buy the fifteen percent from Pagonis," Leander stated, growing more resolved as he located pieces from one of his many plans and modified them to fit this moment. "I will then give you *all* of my shares in Callas as a wedding gift. You will own Callas Cosmetics outright and may run it however you see fit."

Her eyes widened with exhilaration before she dropped her lashes, screening her reaction while she looked to the hands she had arranged in her lap.

"That's an attractive offer, but I don't wish to marry." Her gaze came up again, thoughts shuttered. "At all. It's not personal."

"No?" He thought again of that flash of fear

she had revealed. Was she afraid of all men, not just him? That thought caused an uncomfortable prickle across the back of his shoulders.

Maybe she wasn't into men at all. He didn't see that as an impediment to a marriage for business purposes, though.

"I wouldn't think marriage was something that interests you, either," she said in a remote tone. "You said you don't like people in your space. Ironically, we're a perfect match in that regard. I'm also very private. That's why it's best if we stick to our own corners."

"We could have our own corners," he decided abruptly. "Separate bedrooms."

"A marriage without sex? That *is* a compelling offer." She was being facetious again, the minx.

"I'm serious. I happen to be straight and was under the impression you are, too, but sharing a bed with my wife is not a deal breaker for me." He couldn't believe those words were emerging from his mouth. He loved sex.

He wasn't an opportunist, though. He didn't take whatever was available for the sake of it. Besides, he'd be a fool to trust her. Yes, there was often a power imbalance when a man

brought a woman into his bed, one that typically favored a man, but there were plenty of
men who became ruled by lust. He wouldn't
become one of them.

She tucked her chin, brows coming together
with skepticism. "A marriage in name only?
Really?"

"Disappointed?" he mocked. "Do you want
to have sex with me?"

"Of course not," she said a little too quickly.
"I only met you five minutes ago." Her snip-
piness was the first hint of true emotion she'd
displayed since walking in here. A stain of pink
touched her cheekbones and her gaze slid away
from his. Her spine inched a notch taller.

So defensive and wasn't *that* interesting.

He rubbed the backs of his fingers against
the nap of whiskers under his chin, biting back
a smug grin.

"You don't want children?" he prodded.

Her averted gaze widened as though he'd
sucker punched her. She recovered in a blink
and swiveled her head to look him dead in the
eye.

"No."

Such a lie. One she baldly made straight to

his face. That ought to be ringing all sorts of alarms inside him, but he was far more interested in why she refused to admit she wanted children. He had always assumed he would have a few one day, after he'd achieved the justice he sought.

His desire to marry her took on a new angle, one where he would have the time to pry out all these little secrets and evasions she was hoarding behind her standoffish exterior.

Don't, he warned himself. She was a means to an end. That's all.

"So, it's agreed," he stated, having discovered years ago that those words made his wishes come true. "We'll marry and live in the same home, but within our separate spaces. We'll confine our marital duties to public appearances and hosting events like family dinners…" He grinned in anticipation of that bloodbath.

"It is not agreed," she said, quiet, but firm. "I cannot marry a man who hates me. How can you even consider tying yourself to someone you loathe? Unless the point would be to make my life as uncomfortable as possible?"

"On the contrary," he assured her. "In exchange for switching your allegiance to me, I would provide you with a more comfortable life than ever. You would take full control of your company and all of my wrath would be directed toward the other members of your family."

"Mmm. And I'm sure being extorted into a marriage of revenge would soon provoke my affection toward you." Her pained smile fell away. "But I've thought of a new avenue I can pursue." She rose so abruptly he practically heard the burr of wings in his ears. "Keep your shares. I'll sell mine to my employees. If you then wish to harm the company, you'll be destroying the livelihoods of invested co-owners who have nothing to do with your thirst for vengeance. If you need a referral for a good PR firm to help weather that scandal, I'm happy to provide some names. Thank you for your time today."

"You're really going to walk away from all of this?" The bold black line of her hair down her spine was as enticing as a ribbon to a cat. He wanted to snare it with a claw and drag what was attached into his mouth. "You don't care that I intend to level Pagonis? You'll be impacted, too."

She turned, appearing collected, but he scented

the adrenaline running through her. Her throat flexed as she swallowed and her lips were thin with tension.

"I've already expressed my concern for innocent people. It's a global economy and small disruptions in supply chains can have far-reaching consequences. I would hope you're not so overcome by antipathy you want to cause harm all around the world, but I can't stop you if that's your goal. I certainly don't believe marrying you will give me the power to change your mind."

"What are you going to tell your brother about this meeting, then?"

"Nothing. As I said, my company is the pawn, not me. If you wish to convey a message to him, I'll have my assistant forward his contact details. *Antio sas.*"

Ilona walked straight from his office to the powder room across the lounge. It was as well-appointed and sumptuous as the rest of this top floor with subdued lighting, a selection of her competitor's luxury soaps and lotions, even a change table and a rocking chair suitable for nursing an infant.

She sat down and did her slow breathing exercises, clearing her mind and bringing her heart rate back to normal before she allowed herself to react.

Marriage?

Her heart took a skip and she clenched her eyes shut, counting to ten as she inhaled, then backward as she exhaled.

Marriage wasn't remotely possible, she assured herself. She didn't have to consider it at all. No. She only had to focus on the other piece, where she divested her company to save it. Heartbreaking as that would be, she was proud of arriving at that solution. From a financial and personal standpoint it would be a horrific loss, but she had built it with her own sweat and tears. She could start over with something new. Perhaps she would start a cat café. She could paint cats on the dishes she used to serve spanakopita and souvlaki.

That was such a lovely thought, she actually smiled at her reflection when she rose and dabbed a cool towel at her temples.

She smoothed her hair and examined her makeup. When she was satisfied there was nothing to criticize, she left the powder room, still mentally planning her new life.

"Ah. Good. You're still up here. That saves security detaining you." Leander halted mid-charge from his office. "Tell them to stand down, Androu," he said to the young man who caught himself a hair's breadth before slamming into his boss's back. Leander held Ilona frozen with his sleet-colored gaze. "Let's continue our conversation over lunch."

Ilona fought to speak around the pin that seemed to have punctured her chest. "I have other appointments."

"Advise Kyría Callas's assistant to clear her schedule," Leander told Androu over his shoulder.

"Very good, sir."

Very *not* good, but at least Leander was waving her toward the elevator. Ilona gladly made for the exit, needing out of this building and away from this man.

You don't want children?

Of course, she did. She couldn't take that step right now, though. Not without bringing the hell of Odessa's wrath down upon herself.

"It's not my nature to be obstructive," she told

Leander as the doors closed them into the elevator. "A lifetime of being around domineering men has taught me to pick my battles so I'll go to lunch if you insist, but I won't marry someone who is already demonstrating he wants to control my life."

"It's lunch," he said pithily. "Where we will negotiate the fine points of your taking complete control your company. If yours is anything like mine, it *is* the bulk of your life. Surely that's worth skipping a marketing presentation or whatever you had on."

She wished he would quit dangling the prospect of sole proprietorship. It was a very tasty carrot. The shareholders Leander had recently bought out had been mostly reasonable, but Midas occasionally flexed his influence, backing her into a corner for his own enjoyment. She would love to be free of that.

She would love to be free of Midas. *Love it.*

"You moved your ring," Leander noted.

"Pardon?" She followed his gaze to her right hand where she had reflexively clasped the rail as the elevator plummeted. "Oh." Should she tell him? What would he do with the information? Steal her ring? It wasn't particularly expensive and there was no real way he could weaponize this quirk of hers. "I move it when I want to remember something."

"Such as?" Suspicion narrowed his gaze.

"Picking up my dry cleaning." She lifted a shoulder in an absent shrug. "In this case, I want to remember to look up something when I get home." Clay deposits on Paxos. "I use this ring because it's a coil. I can shrink or expand it for different fingers. If I have more than one thing to remember, I wear it on this finger." She pointed to her index finger. "If it's on this thumb, it's an event I can't miss. If I put it on that one, it's travel."

"Foolish me, paying for an assistant," he said dryly. "So anytime I want to clear your schedule, I can just take that ring?"

"You can try," she shot back, and saw immediately what a mistake it was to challenge him, even mockingly.

Excitement for a wrestle flared in his eyes.

At that exact moment, the elevator dipped below the lobby into an underground parking garage. The glass walls became solid concrete. The lighting changed from bright sunshine to subdued gold, closeting them in intimacy.

The elevator stopped and Leander swayed onto his toes.

He was going to kiss her.

All of her…softened. Her clasp on the rail tightened and her gaze dropped to his mouth. She stood very still, waiting. Wondering. *Wanting…*

CHAPTER THREE

THE DOORS OPENED, releasing all the charged air from this little capsule.

Leander shot his hand out to hold the door and amusement indented the corners of his mouth.

No. She ducked past him, mortified. He knew. He knew she had expected his kiss and now he would use that against her. A meteor shower of fiery ulcers returned to her stomach.

And now she was staring into the open back door of Leander's chauffeured car while her own was at the curb of the lobby above.

"Where shall I have my driver meet me?" she asked stiffly as she slid inside and removed her phone from her bag.

"Dino will take you wherever you wish to go when you're ready."

"The Callas building on Ermou, please," she said promptly. She was *so* done.

"Cute. I'm growing smitten with that sense

of humor of yours," Leander said as he came in beside her and the door slammed. "It's charming."

And there it was. He was taunting her for betraying her attraction. Her chest filled with the hot pressure of helpless persecution and a desire to lash out. She firmly quashed it.

"Take us to that place with the tables, Dino," Leander instructed the driver as he took his seat behind the wheel. "And check the score, would you?"

"Very good, sir." Dino plugged his ears with wireless buds.

Ilona texted her driver to enjoy some personal time and ensured her location was on for her assistant. Then she glanced at her messages and saw Midas wanted her to call. Ugh. She dropped her phone into her clutch.

"You don't seize these moments to be productive?" Leander asked with idle curiosity. His own phone was in his hand, but he seemed to be watching her the way a boxer might study his opponent before climbing into the ring.

"You requested my schedule be cleared. What could possibly be more important than giving you my undivided attention?" she asked to the window as they came up to the street.

"Again with the flirting," he chided.

She turned her head to regard him, trying for a look of infinite patience, but she caught him with his head angled so he could see her ankles.

"What?" She tucked her feet in the other direction and glanced to see if she had scuffed a shoe. Dear heaven, she hadn't paraded through his building with toilet paper stuck to her heel, had she? That really would take the cake. No. She was fine, thank goodness.

"I'm thinking," he murmured as she met his gaze again. There was speculation there, *masculine* speculation.

Ilona knew she was attractive. Her mother had been classically beautiful and Ilona took after her. If anything, she downplayed her looks, but it didn't stop men from coming on to her.

She often wished she had stayed in that awkward stage when she'd had uneven teeth, a flat chest and oversize features on her elfin face. Odessa had reveled in humiliating her over her flaws then, but at least Ilona hadn't been slut-shamed or treated like a sex object.

The older girls at boarding school were responsible for her transformation. They had taken her on as a makeover project, proud of themselves until Ilona finished blossoming with pinup curves and starlet features. At that point she became a rival, whispered about behind jealous hands. Nascent friendships had been cast off in favor of knocking her down.

When she returned home, Odessa had despised and punished Ilona *especially* because she was younger and more beautiful than Odessa would ever be.

Beauty was a form of armor, though. Ilona wore hers at all times and kept it polished to blinding perfection. Which was another reason she had no interest in marriage. Men didn't want her. They only wanted to possess her beauty like a shiny car.

"I honestly can't think of one thing you could offer me that would persuade me to marry you," she informed him.

"Can't you?" His gaze drifted across her features like a caress, settling on her mouth with such intense interest, her lips tingled.

Her heart rate picked up and she rolled her lips inward to press the buzzing out of them.

"No," she choked and snapped her attention forward. Her whole life had been on the wrong side of a seesaw's power imbalance. She wouldn't fill her future with more of it. Her heart constricted at the very thought. "I've explained that I don't wish to be used as a weapon. That goes doubly for being one that's used against myself."

Her stilted words caused a sting of humiliation to crawl up her neck into her cheeks. She couldn't look at him and only hoped he wouldn't play dumb and demand she spell it out further.

After a beat, he said, "You're refreshingly frank."

"Better to call it out than pretend it's not there. That really would allow you to use it as a weapon." Her face was on fire, her chest a cavern of ice, but defensiveness and denial only emphasized a weakness. She'd learned that the hard way.

"You don't see sexual attraction as a weapon *you* can use?"

"On you? Pfft. No." He was far too sophisticated and experienced with seduction. His sexually charged, *I remember her very well* on that phone call when she'd arrived had told her that.

Her sexual experience was confined to rebuffing it. Before him, that had always been relatively easy. Today, she was battling herself. It was distressing to feel so helpless against such a strong attraction. Her gaze kept wanting to swivel back to him and slide all over him. Sitting close to him was agony, making her skin feel tight and prickly. Aware.

She knew he hated her and some puerile part of her wanted him to *like* her, which was self-destructive. She had been taught long ago not to wish for positive regard from people who despised her. That way lay madness.

She smoothed a wrinkle from her skirt, ensuring the hem covered her knee an extra centimeter.

"You've already explained that you'll use any door to debase my family," she said stiffly. "The one to my bedroom is firmly dead bolted. Don't bother knocking."

She expected a tasteless comment about picking her lock. She got profound silence.

She glanced at him.

His features had turned to granite, causing a

small lurch in her chest as she realized she had made a mistake.

"Don't judge me by the standards you're familiar with, Ilona. Unlike your brother, there are certain legal and ethical lines I will never cross."

Had she *insulted* him? That would suggest he cared what she thought of him.

He left her pondering that as they arrived at the restaurant. They were shown through a busy dining room with a full outdoor patio.

It certainly was a place with tables, one so full it would afford them very little privacy.

The host led them to stone stairs and Leander briefly touched her lower back to indicate she should precede him.

With her spine tingling from that innocuous touch, she followed the host upward to a wide breezeway with a half wall that hid them from the dining area below. Here, a half dozen tables were spaced well apart. Between each, tall planters overflowed with fragrant geraniums and colorful petunias. The shade ensured the temperature was several degrees cooler and the din from below was muffled. Plus, they were high enough to see the blue line of the Aegean as well as catch the soft, salt-flavored breeze that floated in from the water.

"This is lovely. I didn't know it existed."

"It's one of my best-kept secrets. Kindly keep it that way. Wine?"

"Light and white, please."

He ordered, requesting the special which was a seafood platter for two.

"Now. Tell me all the reasons you are hesitant to marry me. We've established that bedroom activities will be negotiated separately. What else?"

She opened her mouth, but was briefly too bemused by his assumption to find words.

"Because I don't wish to tie myself to a stranger for the rest of my life," she finally blurted. "Is that something that genuinely appeals to you?"

"It doesn't have to be a lifetime. Ten years would do."

"I'm not throwing away ten years of fertility," she assured him.

"You said you don't want children."

"I don't want children with you," she clarified, grateful the wine arrived. She washed away her fib with a gulp of icy tang flavored with fruit and smoke and a hint of nougat.

Because, as potential mates went, Leander was ridiculously fit for the job. He was healthy and strong, powerful and prosperous, not to mention easy on the eye. At twenty-four, she wasn't in a hurry to start a family, but he was the first man who had made her think seriously about starting one.

He was the first man to make her think about *making* babies.

His eyes narrowed on her and she had the sense he was affronted. She took another gulp, cooling the heat rising in her throat.

"Five years," he suggested.

"That still puts me at thirty before I'm divorced and looking for a suitable father. No."

"Five years, separation after three."

"Are you really willing to go three years without sex? Or are you proposing an open arrangement?" She didn't know why she asked. Yes, she did. Because it would humiliate her to sit at home while he was out getting his jollies with someone else. For the first time in her life, she felt a pinch of empathy for Odessa, forced to

raise the consequence of her husband's habit-
ual wandering eye.

"We'll keep it simple." Leander made every
statement sound as though it was an agreed decision that would go into a contract they were
negotiating. "No affairs. Yes, I'm confident
I can survive three years without sex. Why?
What's your record?"

Twenty-four years and four months, not that
it was any of his business.

"I honestly don't understand how you see this
marriage benefiting you," she said with fray-
ing patience. "What would you gain beyond
the ability to make my life difficult? I am not
Midas, Leander. If you want to punish him,
please highjack him into lunch and invite him
to partake in your honeymoon of celibacy."

"What I will get, *glykiá mou*, is your shares
in Pagonis," he explained with exaggerated patience and a self-satisfied smile. "They will be
your wedding gift to *me*."

"So you can dismantle and destroy the company my father's grandfather started? I already
told you I think that's awful. I won't facilitate
it."

"I'm not asking you to." He sobered. "You

made your point. Harming the workforce is poor justice and it won't cause Midas to lose any sleep. No. I'll use my influence to oust him instead."

"As president? I admire your optimism, but if my portion in Pagonis afforded that sort of influence, I would have done it myself by now."

"No, you wouldn't. You said you pick your battles and you clearly don't want one with him. I have more of a taste for blood. If someone picks a battle with me, I stay in it until I win."

She didn't doubt that for a second. If she wasn't very careful, she would wind up married to him despite her best effort to avoid it.

"Be honest," he cajoled. "Who would you rather see running Pagonis? Midas or me?"

"That's not a fair question. I don't know you." She rolled the stem of her wineglass between her fingers, considering what she had read about him, once she had realized he was buying up shares in her company. Leander had seemed to innovate his way to the top of his field. He had taken big risks and leapt on opportunities—like shares in her company—but there weren't any whiffs of bribery or other heinous tactics.

Unlike Midas, who was capable of anything.

"Is your recipe for low-carbon cement really yours?" she asked.

"There you go lumping me in with your brother again." Leander curled his lip. "I don't steal my innovations. I develop them myself. Answer my question."

"I'm thinking." She was thinking about having complete control over Callas without Midas interfering. She was thinking about Midas facing a comeuppance that was long overdue. Dear heaven, that was such a tempting vision.

However.

"You're right. I don't want a fight with Midas. He makes a ferocious enemy, as you must know. I'm not actually an object, Leander. Do you realize that? You want me to be your blade or bullet or *pawn*. That's not how Midas will see it. He will see it as a betrayal. All this anger you have toward him will be gathered up by Midas and turned onto me. There is no win for me in what you're proposing. At least while Callas is under the Pagonis umbrella, I have some protection."

"I'm not going to let anyone, least of all that bastard, come after my wi—" Leander sat back, mouth setting into a grim line as his laser-sharp gaze fixed on something over her shoulder. "Speak of the devil. Did you tell him where we were?"

"Who? Midas?" Her heart came into her mouth and a wash of ice water went through her, stilling all the what-ifs and maybes that she had allowed to swirl inside her. She didn't turn to look, saying woodenly, "My assistant likely did."

"Why?" Leander's infuriated gaze stayed on his enemy, but she felt his anger flaring out to encompass her, eroding the small degree of respect she'd earned from him.

It was startlingly painful to feel his regard yanked away so abruptly.

"Hey," an American man called from one of the other tables. "My wife is using that. She's coming right back."

Ilona turned her head to see Midas was ignoring the American and coming at them with a stolen chair. He set it backward at their table and straddled it as he sat, arms folded across the back. His glare of bitter accusation fell over Ilona like a jar over a spider.

He looked so much like their father from his

square face to his barrel chest, it was always disconcerting to see stark hatred thrown at her from features that had usually worn an expression of patronizing fondness.

She forced herself to meet Midas's filthy look with an impassive one, but her pulse was galloping and a fizz of alarm shot through her when Leander abruptly stood. Was he *leaving*? Well, that was just great, wasn't it?

Leander handed his chair to the man who'd chased Midas. Then Leander folded his arms and looked down his nose at both of them.

Ilona had to admire how neatly he had turned the tables on Midas's attempt at a power grab. Perhaps he *was* strong enough to take on the bane of her existence.

If he was, that was a caution in itself, one she should heed.

"I told Feodor that you should call me," Midas said without preamble.

"I got that message, but I'm having lunch with my new partner in Callas." She waved at Leander.

Midas didn't look at him. His cheek ticked with barely suppressed rage.

"Why? Rideaux is rallying the board members, insisting we sell our Callas shares to him." He jerked his head at Leander. "I told Rideaux to hang tight because you had promised to counter. That is what you're doing, isn't it?" The threat in his voice poured terror into her blood.

But she saw immediately—*immediately*—that Midas had lied when he had said he would accept her counteroffer for the Pagonis shares. His goal was to instigate a bidding war between her and Leander. He didn't care who got the shares in the end so long as the price went up, filling his coffers before he cut her loose completely.

No wonder he was incensed to find her conspiring with Leander.

How could she still be so naive that she had missed the depth of his avarice?

"Tell me you are not cutting a deal with him, Ilona," Midas said grimly. He would never let her forget this. Never. She wanted to cry at Leander. *See what you've done?* But Leander wouldn't care that he had called this punishment down upon her. In his mind, she was a Pagonis and deserved nothing but pain.

She wanted to run. Literally run away, but she

was cornered both physically and figuratively. Midas sat on the chair and Leander stood in the space to the left of the table, both blocking her into the end of the breezeway.

"Ilona and I have been discussing options," Leander said. "She has made clear that she doesn't wish to be used as a pawn or a weapon against you."

A contemptuous curl arrived at the corner of Midas's mouth, one that said, *I knew it.* Pathetic little Ilona, too afraid of him to betray him.

"I've assured her that I wouldn't dream of putting my wife in such a position," Leander continued.

"What?" Midas finally snapped his attention up to Leander.

What? Ilona's heart nearly fell out of her mouth.

"Ilona and I are getting married," Leander stated, holding Midas's gaze while thrusting out a hand to her.

"That is not true." Midas's hand curled into a fist on the back of the chair. "Is it, Ilona?"

A choice had to be made. Stick with the devil she knew or align with a new one.

The waves were crashing and frothing angrily below, but it suddenly struck her that *she* was the doll. *She* was on fire, slowly being scorched and damaged and turned to ash.

There was only one way to douse those flames. *Leap.*

She rose and accepted Leander's hand. Her heart exploded with trepidation as the ground fell away from beneath her.

Leander was right there, pulling her into the solid wall of his body as though he could shelter her from the impact.

"Between us, we have a majority in Callas," Leander was saying to Midas. "My offer for the fifteen percent stands, but tell the board to sell it to whomever they wish. We don't need it."

Menace darkened Midas's complexion. "You're making a mistake, Ilona."

She couldn't speak. She was in that disorienting, breathless place where sound was muffled and everything had become a blur. She couldn't tell which way was up.

Leander's arm was crushing her. Maybe that's why she couldn't breathe, but his firm grip told her she wasn't in this cold, airless place alone. She let her arm slide behind his back, clasping on to him while she searched for something to say.

"Excuse us," Leander said dismissively. "We're celebrating."

"I bet you are." Midas jerked to his feet, toppling his chair and leaving it where it fell against the stones.

As he walked away, he met the waiter with the platter of seafood they had ordered. Midas knocked it out of the man's hand, raining shrimp and calamari onto the patrons below.

He ignored the shouts of anger and kept walking.

A surge of triumph had Leander barking out a laugh and throwing both his arms around his *fiancée*, squeezing her lithe form while he started to plant an exuberant kiss—

She went stiff with rejection. Her face had drained so her complexion was more olive than honey-gold. Her arm was bent against his chest, not pushing him away, but tense enough to hold him off. Her thick black lashes were lowered to hide her eyes, but her mouth was tight with anxiety.

She was trembling so hard, a different compulsion rocked through him, the kind that wanted to cradle her close. He smoothed his hand over her narrow back, disconcerted to realize she was much slighter than she seemed. The way beauty radiated off her created a halo of presence that was bigger than she physically was.

"Are you going to faint?" he asked with concern.

"Of course not. But I've lost my appetite. I'd like to leave." She extricated herself from his hold and reached for her handbag on the edge of the table.

Somehow, her hand took a wild lurch and knocked over her glass of wine.

Her inhale was a sharp tear of sound. He braced for a scream to come out of her, but she only stared at the spreading stain, body so taut he thought one touch would cause her to shatter.

She carefully released her breath and looked at his shirt button. Her mouth was quivering, her eyes unblinking. "I'll find my own way back."

"I'll take you."

She didn't argue, only started for the stairs.

The server met them there and assured them their meal would be remade immediately.

"We're leaving. Bill me for our meal and for all the guests who were affected. Allow them to order anything else they wish." Leander left Androu's number for the invoice.

As they slid into his vehicle, he was still hungry for food, still thirsty for blood. Still grimly gratified, but wondering if he had overplayed his hand. It had been very satisfying to watch his enemy take that kick to the stomach, but he would have preferred to spring the marriage on Midas when it was a fait accompli.

The way Ilona was reacting had him wondering if she would try to back out.

"What made you side with me?" he asked curiously.

She was bringing her phone to her ear and held up a trembling finger. Her voice was unsteady as she said, "It's me— Yes, I know, Feodor. I just saw him. No, that's fine."

"Is that your assistant? *Fire him*," Leander said in a spark of temper. Everything he'd been trying to do today had been jeopardized by Midas showing up in the middle of it. If Androu had ever revealed his whereabouts without his consent, he would know he was terminated before Leander had to think the words.

Ilona ignored him. "Tell Eugene to make a code yellow adjustment and meet me at the curb in fifteen minutes. Do that now, then come back to me." She angled the phone away from her mouth. "Please take me to my office, Dino. I mean it this time."

"Yes, *kyría*." Dino pulled out and headed east.

"I don't expect my employees to stand between me and my family," Ilona told Leander. "Feodor knows to be as circumspect as possible, but Midas would only install spies in my company if he didn't get the information he wants when he wants it. Feodor weighs the cost benefit and— Yes, I'm here." She went back to her call. "I need to meet with accounting and legal as soon as I'm in the building. See if you can get my own accountant and lawyer into a room in the next day or two. I also want to speak with the property agent who found my flat."

"I have a property agent," Leander interjected. "We'll meet with her together to find a house that suits us both."

He should be on his own phone, telling Androu to set up his own meetings, but he was morbidly fascinated by Ilona's swiftness to action. Disturbingly, it reminded him of those initial hours after he'd found his father, when his mind had been crystal clear and he'd done all the things so fast he couldn't even remember how the emergency personnel had been notified or his father's body removed. He'd come back to awareness two weeks later, rocked out of his stupor to realize he was in a utility vehicle rambling across the tundra without any recollection of how his father had been laid to rest or who had tried to console him.

"Hold a moment, Feodor." She lowered the phone. "We can meet with your agent, but I need mine for something else. What is our timeline? Do you want a proper wedding? I don't. They take ages to organize and I'd prefer something quiet since this isn't—"

"Short timeline, big splash," he stated. "Weeks not months. I'll arrange the wedding if you don't want to."

She made a face and went back to her assistant. "I need you to hire a wedding planner—" Something Feodor said broke through her shield and she gave a bemused shake of her head. "You're such a cliché sometimes. Yes, take the lead, but you can't do it all yourself. I have a lot to accomplish in the next short while so hire a professional planner and— Pardon? Oh, it's, um…" Her stark expression slid to Leander. The pinpoints of her pupils exploded to swallow the dark brown of her irises. "I'm marrying Leander Vasilou."

Her words struck in his ears like a hammer, reverberating through his whole being. He was doing this. Marrying her. A Pagonis.

He didn't even know if he could trust her. A phrase he'd heard his English mother once use emerged from his suppressed childhood. *Marry in haste, repent at leisure.*

"Almost there," Ilona said, peering forward. "Send my private number to Leander's assistant. I'll see you in a moment." She ended the call and dropped her phone into her clutch.

Callas Cosmetics had manufacturing facilities around the world, but its head office and research laboratory were still located in its original building, one that Ilona had taken over from a long-defunct textile plant, revitalizing a depressed area into upscale industry.

Dino drew to a halt outside the glass-fronted entrance and left the car, coming around to Leander's door where he waited for Leander's signal before opening it.

At the same time, a nondescript man in a dark suit emerged from the lobby. He had a hand to his ear as he spoke through an earpiece to some unseen party.

"You ordered an escort into the building?" Code yellow explained. Leander scanned an alert gaze up and down the block. "Are you concerned Midas will confront you here?"

"He'll send Hercules first. Maybe Odessa." She clamped both hands over the top of her clutch. "I don't know if you realize what you have unleashed, Leander. Don't let his name fool you. Midas turns everything he touches to poison, not gold."

"I know." His chest tightened as his mind conjured his last glimpse of his father. "Is that why you sided with me? You consider me the lesser of two evils?"

She ran restless hands over the smooth patent leather of her bag, seeming to choose her words carefully.

"With respect, I sided with myself. As long as

my father was alive, and Pagonis International owned a piece of my company, I was forced to maintain positive relations with Midas. Today, you offered me a way to sever ties. I took it. I *will* take it." Her eyes were hollow caves, her cheekbones like tent poles beneath gaunt drapes. "I'm under no illusion that you won't cut me loose if it serves your purpose. I'm prepared to do the same if it comes down to a choice between you or me."

"We continue to prove how well suited we are," he drawled.

"Will you let me out, please? People are waiting for me."

Leander knocked on the window and Dino opened the door. Leander rose and helped Ilona from the car. Her hand was pure ice in his.

He held on to it for an extra second, preventing her from walking away, forcing her to glance questioningly at him.

"I'll collect you for dinner at seven."

"If you'd like," she said in the tone that said she picked her battles and had no desire to engage in this one. "I'll see you then."

CHAPTER FOUR

ILONA WAS EXHAUSTED from a day of sustained stress made worse by pretending she was over-joyed about a marriage she had deep reservations about agreeing to.

By the time she was dressing for dinner, all she wanted to do was crawl into a bath and go to bed early. She wanted to lock the door of her flat and stay here forever, rather than march forward on the path she'd charted.

She still couldn't tell if she had exercised agency or pushed the self-destruct button on her life. It had been enormously satisfying to get the better of Midas—for about three seconds. Which was about how long her actions would impact him. He *would* retaliate and the dread of waiting to learn what form it would take was agonizing.

She might have withstood his attack, might have been able to take every precaution and feel protected against him, but she had this other unprotected flank—the one she'd exposed to Leander.

If she had wanted to finally take on Midas, she really ought to have chosen a partner she could trust. Instead, she'd made a bargain with a complete stranger—one who was equally powerful and dangerous and had a grudge against her.

In fact, he was *more* dangerous to her. Rather than intimidate her into doing things she didn't want to do, he had *enticed* her. He had inspired her with his complete lack of fear where Midas was concerned, making her believe in his strength. In her own.

But her mind kept wanting to go back to that moment at the restaurant when she had stood and grasped his hand. If only she could push Undo. Nothing about this felt safe. It felt like the longest long shot and she had never been a gambler.

There was no going back, though. The scene at the restaurant had turned the paparazzi's interest on to them. Her PR department was already fielding calls asking if their association was business or romantic.

Whatever happened from now on would play

out under a relentless spotlight of media attention so she took extra care with her appearance, expecting to be photographed with Leander tonight. Her midlength dress was a figure-hugging satin slip with an emerald-green lace overlay. An onyx clip over her left ear held her hair off her face, but she left the rest loose. She added drama to her eyes and lips and slipped on shoes that were an inch taller than her typical day wear.

The doorman called up as she was moving her things into her evening clutch, informing her that Hercules had arrived to see her.

Right on time, she thought dourly.

"I'll meet him in the lobby." In the past, she had let Hercules up, but not today. Not for the foreseeable future.

Hercules was two years younger than she was and had once been a wellspring of affection toward her, back when they'd been small enough to snuggle while watching cartoons. Eventually, he had been forced to choose, though. His mother didn't care for rivals, especially when it came to the men in her life. Ilona didn't blame Hercules for taking the less painful route of allowing Ilona to be the target of censure so he didn't have to be, but it still hurt.

She felt for him, though. He hadn't had the chance to prove himself to their father before Apollo Pagonis had died. It had been an uphill battle anyway. Apollo had fostered an atmosphere of competition among his children, promising the most successful would run the corporation he'd inherited from his own father. Midas had been several years ahead of them and had stolen Leander's technology to win that race. Ilona had come a close second with her honestly earned cosmetic enterprise—even if that had always been seen as a folly of little consequence.

Hercules had the soul of an artist. He had struggled with economics and spreadsheets, compromising by turning his talents to marketing, but his heart wasn't in it. He suffered in lonely silence on the inside of the wall that separated her from being a "real" Pagonis.

Tonight, he was more melancholy than usual. His shoulders were a sloped line, his mop of Technicolor hair mussed by his own hand. His eyes flashed wide with persecution as he spotted her coming off the elevator and he rushed forward.

"Ilona. *What* are you doing?"

"I have a date," she said, deliberately misunderstanding him.

Hercules dipped his head to speak in a low voice. "He'll make your life a living hell. You know that, don't you?" He was speaking about Midas and shot a look to the doorman behind his desk, as if that man would report him for speaking ill of his brother. "I can't protect you this time."

"How is that different from the status quo?" she asked with a blink.

His features tightened. "That's not fair. You don't know what I do."

No, she didn't. She experienced another pang that he might have tried in the past to help her and yet his efforts remained invisible. Ineffectual. How demoralizing for both of them.

"Now you don't have to put yourself out," she said gently. "My car is here," she noted as Dino halted outside and Leander stepped out.

"Ilona." Hercules grabbed her arm as she started to brush by. "*Not him.* Not like this.

Midas was *incensed*. So was Mother," he added abstractly.

Because marriage meant children. Ilona *should* get pregnant with Leander's baby. There would be a macabre delight in tormenting Odessa with that nightmare scenario.

"Ask Midas why *not* Leander," she advised. "Excuse me. I don't want to keep my fiancé waiting."

Hercules tightened his grip while Leander yanked open the door into the lobby and asked in a lethal voice, "Do you need help, Ilona?"

"No," she said mildly while his tone caused her heart to crash around in her chest like a loose cannonball.

"You don't even know him," Hercules accused as he released her. "What makes you think you'll be better off with him? Ask *him* why *you*."

She already knew why her. And no, his motives weren't lily white, but at least he'd been up-front with her about them. She ignored Hercules and walked outside where she manufactured a smile for Dino as he opened the car door for her. She stole a calming breath as she slipped inside.

"Are you all right?" Leander asked as he came in behind her.

"Perfectly," she lied because what was the use in admitting she was petrified? Hercules might not be very good at protecting her, but he was never wrong when he forewarned her.

"Did you read the press release?" Leander asked her as they got underway.

"I did. That date will work." Even though it meant she had only three short weeks of freedom before she walked into a new cage. *What* was she doing with her life?

"I'll tell Androu." Leander placed the call as they drove. That didn't surprise her. He was locking her into her decision. She understood that. It compressed the air in her lungs, but there was no going back. She knew that, too.

"Excellent news," Leander said as he finished his call and tucked his phone away. "After he left us, Midas tried to stop my purchase of your shares. Rideaux squeezed another two percent out of me, but I only gave it on condition he rally the board by midnight. He rammed it through and those shares will be yours on our wedding day."

"That is good news." She forced the corners

of her mouth upward. "My lawyer is working on the language to give you control of my shares in Pagonis. I can't give them to you outright, but I can designate you to manage them and vote in my stead. She'll forward my terms for the prenuptial agreement to your lawyer by the end of the week. For the most part, I suggest we retain the property we bring to the marriage so we'll only have to split what we acquire jointly, like the house we purchase to share."

"Agreed."

So civilized.

Ilona supposed she should be grateful, but she had always imagined that if she did marry, it would be driven by a burning desire to be with that other person. Trust would be so deeply ingrained in the relationship, cold details like contracts and conditions for their divorce would be completely absent from the process.

Next time, she assured herself ironically while also feeling a pang that this marriage was temporary. He didn't really want her and that was so much like the rest of her family, it scored deep lines behind her heart.

They arrived at the restaurant on Lycabettus Hill and caused a small stir as they were shown onto the terrace. Their table overlooked the twinkle of the city, the glowing Parthenon and the three-quarter moon casting its light on the smooth Aegean.

"Our reputation precedes us," she murmured as he helped her with her light wrap. "I don't suppose anyone will notice the view tonight."

"I certainly won't. You look lovely. Are you cold? Would you like to keep this?"

His casual compliment and the brush of his touch against her shoulders had caused goose bumps to rise on her skin.

Discomfited, she murmured, "I'm fine."

He handed off her wrap to the hovering maître d' before he held her chair for her.

Between his solicitous gesture and the melody of stringed instruments and the soft breeze, this was the most romantic date she'd ever been on. Yet it wasn't that at all, she acknowledged with a pinch of melancholy.

Leander studied her as he took his seat, gaze delving into hers while his expression remained inscrutable.

"Second thoughts?" he asked as though he

could read past the serene mask she had learned to wear in self-protection.

Her pulse tripped, but she pressed a light smile onto her lips. "And third, fourth and fifth. You?"

"None."

His resolve made her nerves jangle.

"Shall we make this official?" he asked.

"I thought our lawyers were doing that?"

"I mean this." He reached into his jacket pocket and set a velvet box beside the small lantern between them.

"Oh." Her breath rushed out of her and, inexplicably, the backs of her eyes stung.

Gasps rose from nearby tables. Her throat went dry and she clenched her hands in her lap, but there was nothing to grasp on to. Her grip on her previous life was gone.

"You know how to keep an audience in suspense, don't you?" he murmured when she only stared at the tiny box. "I was going to ask you to pick it yourself, but when I saw that it reminded me of the ring you were wearing this morning. See what you think."

Had it only been this morning that they'd met and agreed to this caper?

To her mortification, her hands were visibly shaking as she reached for it. She heard another ripple of amused emotion travel through their audience.

How excruciating. She was a private person at the best of times and now everyone saw how she was reacting. *He* saw it.

She pried the box open and a dazzling marquise-cut diamond flashed like an arc weld into her eye. It was bridged over a spiral band of pavé-set diamonds, echoing the style of her day ring.

"It's beautiful." She was nearly struck speechless, unable to think of the last time she had received a gift of any kind, let alone something so lovely and personal. Something she instantly adored with her whole heart.

"It should fit. Your assistant really does give up too much of your personal information." He pinched the ring to remove it from the box, then held out his other hand in request for hers.

His warm fingers cradled the fine bones of her hand and the cool weight slid up her finger, nestling into place as though it belonged there. A signal seemed to pulse from the flashing stone all the way up her arm to spark in her chest.

"No moving this one," he said with a light tap against her knuckle. "It stays here to remind you that I'm in your life."

As if she could forget! It was such a patently silly thing to suggest, a day's worth of tension sputtered out of her in befuddled laughter.

His remote expression altered, softening into something that made her heart skip and the rest of her say, *Oh.*

Then applause rose around them, reminding her they were under intense scrutiny.

She started to withdraw her hand from his, but some joker started clinking a knife against a glass in that annoying demand for a groom to kiss his bride.

"Shall we?" Leander kept her hand and stood to draw her to her feet.

Did they have to? Sex was off the table, but they hadn't said anything about kissing. She could have demurred. She could have done anything, but she let him draw her to him.

Goodness, he was tall! She was five-eight and wore three-inch heels, but he still towered over her. His broad shoulders blocked her from most of the prying eyes, which was a small relief, but his arms were sliding around her, gathering her close. His gaze held hers as his head dipped.

Her lips softened and parted as his mouth arrived…at the corner of hers.

That might have been all it was, but she accidentally turned the two millimeters needed so her mouth was under his. She lifted her chin to invite more. More pressure. More heat. More of the swirling fog that closed over her as he waited a single beat before his mouth sealed firmly over hers, commanding and suddenly hungry.

She hadn't realized she was calling up a storm. His arms firmed around her as his tongue dabbed, then he devoured her. It wasn't the taking of a ferocious wind that stripped her naked, though. It felt a little like that. She was bowed and defenseless against an unseen force, but in the same way he had coaxed her to detonate her own life, he brought forth a burst of sensuality from within her. She was suddenly soaked in need. In *yearning*. In a compulsion to lean into the wildness and become part of it.

As sensations rocked and ripped through her,

she lost track of where she was. She swayed and clung to his strength, reveling in the movement of his hands across her back, giving herself up to this plundering kiss. His strength was all that held her up and, for a few moments, she felt safe here, even as every ounce of her self-possession was incinerated.

Joyful laughter and applause penetrated, reminding her they were in public.

She wanted to cringe away, then. Hopefully, he would believe she was only playing her part the same way he must be. *He* hadn't completely abandoned his pride, though. Only her. How debasing.

"Will you let me go, please?" she asked into his throat.

"I can't," he growled. "My cuff link is caught in the lace of your dress. Also, your lipstick is smudged. Is it all over my mouth?"

She dared a glance upward. What a depressing comedy of errors.

She stole his pocket square and, staying close against the shelter of his chest, surreptitiously swept the linen around the border of her lips. She lifted her lashes in question.

"Better," he assured her and took it with his

free hand. He scrubbed it across his own mouth before he thrust it into the side pocket of his jacket.

Then he peered over her shoulder, arms encircling her as he carefully untangled himself.

She belatedly realized what was pressed against her stomach. His erection.

A bolt of shocked delight—and shock that she was delighted—went through her. Perhaps he hadn't been faking the passion in his kiss?

He released her and cool air swirled across her overheated skin. He helped her with her chair and used the drape of his jacket to hide his fly as he retook his seat.

She might have sat there in a state of complete shock, but a server arrived with champagne. The cork popped and please, *please* let that be the last time the rest of the diners clapped and cheered.

"To us," Leander said as they touched the rims of their tall flutes.

She drank hers way too fast.

CHAPTER FIVE

LEANDER HADN'T SEEN ILONA since their engagement dinner two nights ago. After their passionate kiss, she had steered their conversation to pedestrian topics like a tentative guest list and their preferences for a house. They had said their good-nights outside her building without another kiss or an invitation to join her upstairs—not that he had expected one, previous, mind-blowing kiss notwithstanding.

That kiss had kept him hard nearly every minute since, however. It had been meant as a brief stamp of finality on their deal, but she had turned her head ever so slightly and her mouth had melted like spun sugar beneath his own. Who knew a kiss could catch fire? Not him, but in seconds a conflagration had surrounded them.

He had stood within it, reveled in it, while her lithe body pressed against his in surrender.

If he hadn't felt his cuff become snared in her dress, he might be kissing her still.

But he had and that had been a necessary moment of sanity.

Even so, he wondered through the next hours and days if they really would eschew sex when they had such incredible chemistry. He wasn't a masochist so why torture himself if she was amenable?

Thirty minutes ago, he had received his answer. His head of PR had tipped him off to a rumor circulating about his intended. He didn't want to believe it, but it would explain why Ilona had leapt on his proposal so unexpectedly and kissed him with such fervor.

Did she think he was born yesterday? What he had briefly forgotten was that she was a Pagonis. They were born without a conscience.

The question was, would he go through with marrying her to achieve what he wanted despite the way she was trying to pull the wool over his eyes?

"There she is." Ursula, his property agent, noted Ilona's car was approaching up the drive of the villa they were here to view.

When the car halted, Leander opened the

back door himself. Ilona's calf and half her thigh briefly flashed from the slit in her skirt, sending an irritating jolt of heat into his groin.

He didn't *want* to respond to her, but now that he'd had that brief taste, he couldn't help it. Everything about her appealed to his basest instincts, making him want to touch and taste and explore and own.

As she straightened, she started to slip on her sunglasses, but he stopped her.

"We'll be inside. You don't need those." He stole them and dropped them into the backseat, wanting to see every thought and machination that crossed her deceptive heart.

A hundred emotions glinted and sparked in the melted chocolate of her irises, from surprise to nervous searching of his gaze to wary vulnerability. Her lashes flickered as she dropped her attention to his mouth, seeming to expect a greeting.

He was tempted to kiss the hell out of her. Would she give herself up in the same way every time? He was dying to know, but he confined himself to a brief brush of his lips against her cheek.

Erotic memory wafted into his brain with the

subtle fragrance of anise and roses that clung to her skin, enticing him, but he didn't give in.

"Meet Ursula," he said abruptly.

Ilona's mouth might have briefly trembled in rejection, but he was learning that she had a talent for overcoming moments of transparency. It was as maddening as it was admirable, but it was also a reason to be cautious, reminding him she kept a lot hidden.

"It's nice to meet you." She shook the agent's hand.

Leander walked behind them as Ursula escorted Ilona inside and extolled the virtues of the property. The neighborhood of Ekali was a prime location and this terraced estate was very private, surrounded by trees while still affording mountain views from its tiers of verandas and balconies.

They paused in the foyer where black-and-white tiles were arranged in concentric circles beneath a dome that poured sunlight onto the wide spiral staircase. Grand archways ensured the entire ground level flowed from one room into another. An airy lounge became a music room and then a dining area. At the back, a wall of glass opened onto the garden and further along, the pool.

Ursula knew Leander well. She mentioned the indoor pool and the servants' quarters in the lower floor, then wrapped up her pitch, suggesting they explore the rest on their own.

That suited him. He wanted a private word with his fiancée.

Ilona was quiet as they returned to the main staircase and walked up, but he sensed her glancing surreptitiously at him from beneath her lashes.

A second, equally splendid spiral took them to the top floor which was completely reserved as a master suite with separate bedrooms, each with its own bath. A small lounge connected the two rooms. The house was built into a hillside, so there was a walk-out to an upper garden along with a balcony that overlooked the pool.

As they squinted against the sunshine, assessing the view, Leander considered whether to ask her outright if she was using him to hide an unplanned pregnancy or whether it was better to feed her enough rope to hang herself.

"I think it's perfect," Ilona said in the exceedingly polite tone he found so unsatisfying.

"Really? I hate it." He really did. There were too many stairs, too much deliberate opulence. It was both claustrophobic with the surrounding trees, and yet had a view that was uninspiring. Also, he was in a very bad mood, uninclined to like anything.

Ilona jerked at his antagonistic tone, but quickly recovered. "We're being honest?"

"I expect honesty at all times," he shot back.

Her chin briefly wobbled before she firmed it, but she held his gaze without flinching.

"Very well. I see value in the fact it's available immediately. It meets our basic requirement for separate bedrooms and a convenient location to our work. If we close today, we won't have to waste time on further searching. I don't love the decor, but it will impress guests and has enough room for entertaining large crowds. It's not meant to be our home, only something we'll occupy for three years, so perhaps I should have said, 'It will do.'"

Three years. She wasn't looking for a father to actually raise her child, only support it and give it a name?

"'Large crowds?'" he repeated. "What happened to not wanting people in your space?"

"I thought entertaining was a legal requirement once you marry. While my father was alive, my stepmother threw dinner parties two or three times a week. She had several larger holiday bashes and charity galas throughout the year."

"Good God. Is that something you want to do?"

"Not in the least. After a busy day at work, I might entertain the neighbor's cat, but that's about all the interaction I'm up for."

Not the neighbor. The neighbor's *cat*. He didn't let himself be diverted by that whimsical little revelation, but he did enjoy it.

"I typically buy out a restaurant when I'm required to host anything. Or use my yacht."

"We could continue to do that. Or..." She went back inside where she looked around thoughtfully. "We could buy this as an investment. It could serve as a venue for our own events, but villas like this are in demand for destination weddings. It could provide an income when we don't need it."

That was actually a solid proposal.

"*We* could marry here," she continued, brightening. "Feodor would love that. He's having trouble finding a suitable location."

"Seriously, why do you keep him?" Leander asked with exasperation. "He seems completely incompetent."

She paused at the top of the stairs, jaw slack. Then her chin came up.

"It's not his fault. My stepmother keeps undermining him. She threatened two designers with ruin if they worked with me and fired one of her favorite caterers from a standing lunch contract simply because they submitted a quote for our reception."

"Which sounds like they're available. Where's the problem?" he drawled.

"That's not the point I'm making." She started down the stairs. "Odessa is going out of her way to be obstructive. As I just explained, she made a career of entertaining. She knows everyone and put the word out that she will punish those who work on—or attend—our wedding. The invitations haven't even gone out, but Feodor has already received a dozen regrets."

"Why would she do that?" He moved to catch up with her, expecting Midas was behind it.

"Because she can. My relationship with her

has always been difficult." Her lashes shielded her eyes as she continued downward.

"Why?" He kept his tone conversational, taking all of this with a grain of salt. She was clearly trying to discredit her stepmother in order to undermine any rumors that had reached his ears from that quarter.

"Why do you think? My father had an affair with my mother and, when she died, had the bright idea of insisting Odessa raise his bastard alongside her legitimate sons." Her profile was the deep carving of a cameo, still and sharp.

She stopped again and released a hiss of consternation.

He paused two steps lower so he was eye level when she pensively bit her bottom lip, reminding him how plump and lush it had tasted when he had roamed his tongue across it.

Why the hell did she have to be *so* enticing and *so* impossible to trust?

"I should tell you..." Her throat flexed. "Odessa is spreading some very ugly rumors about me. The most tasteless is that I'm pregnant. She's telling people that's why we're rushing this marriage, but that it's not even yours."

And there it was. She was attempting to get

ahead of it by telling him herself, but he steeled himself against giving her any sort of credit for that.

"Are you?" he asked, forcing a tone of vague interest.

"Pregnant? No!" She was taken aback. Then, as she read his skepticism, her mouth pressed into a line of grim resignation. "I see. This isn't new information. You already heard it and you believe it."

"She knows you better than I do." He canted his head. "I'd be a fool to discount it, especially given how quickly you agreed to marry me. If something seems too good to be true, it usually is."

"You think this marriage looks too good to be true? Pah!" She moved across the step, intending to brush past him.

He shifted to block her path.

Ilona pulled up short and straightened her spine, trying to look down her nose at him, but she wasn't quite tall enough for it to have an effect. Plus, her heart was racing at this confrontation and her head was about to explode. It was taking all her effort to maintain control of herself and not start to cry. True disdain was beyond her.

"If I were pregnant, I wouldn't have agreed to a celibate marriage," she pointed out. "Even a sucker who snaps up Odessa's lies like they're shares in Callas Cosmetics could figure out he wasn't the father if I never had sex with him."

"But you kissed me like you wanted to have sex on the table of the restaurant," he reminded her in a mockingly helpful tone.

Humiliation stabbed into the spot beneath her throat. She knew she was going red with guilt and shame, but she'd been attacked by sarcasm and false accusations enough that she kept her temper. Barely. Her voice shook when she spoke.

"It sounds as though you also bought the one where I'm a whore who gets her kicks by breaking up marriages. I genuinely don't care what you think of me, Leander, but let me assure you, there is *nothing* that could induce me to raise a child in a household where one parent resents them. Would you excuse me, please?"

She returned to the inside of the step and this time he let her pass. She reached the bottom and hurried her way across the foyer to the lounge where Ursula stood outside the windows, pacing in the shade of a tree as she spoke on her phone.

Leander came up behind her, but she refused to look back to see what was on his face. She held her arms crossed, but ensured her tense shoulders remained down and back, not hunched and defensive the way she wanted to pull them.

"Dumping me now will do nothing to hurt Midas," she pointed out, barely turning her head. "He'll dance a jig over my public disgrace, but that is the only effect it will have. Do whatever appeases that sickness inside you, though. I knew I couldn't count on you." She had contingency plans in place. Her agent hadn't found her a property yet, but she was looking.

"I didn't say I was dumping you." He arrived beside her at the window, hands shoved into his pockets. "I said I expect honesty."

She choked on a laugh of disbelief. "You don't believe a word I say! What does it matter if I tell you the truth or not?"

"You switched sides without remorse. It follows that you have ulterior motives."

"I told you what they were—to sever ties with them. I hate them more than you do."

"I doubt that."

"Of course, you do. Again, what's the point in telling you the truth if you presume I'm lying?" The backs of her eyes were hot and a scalded line sat behind her breastbone. It was the familiar ache of her feelings being dismissed and ignored. Disbelieved.

She sensed him looking at her, sensed his frustration that she would throw his words back in his face like that. Did he expect her to grovel and beg him to believe her? Been there, done that, had the emotional scars to prove it.

After a long minute, he grimly acknowledged, "This *is* war. They were bound to try to divide us."

Another choke of disparaging laughter escaped her. "I hate to dent your ego, Leander, but this isn't about you. I mean, Midas is always thrilled when Odessa makes my life difficult, but she's not doing it for him."

"Why then?"

There was an agonizing wrench in her chest. "It doesn't matter," she decided wearily.

"It sounds like it does matter. If you want me

to trust you and believe what you say, tell me the truth, Ilona."

Persecution had her glaring her astonishment at him, wondering why he insisted on turning the knife within her.

"I *am* telling you the truth," she said on a burst of bitter outrage. "I was a child who was given no choice in where I went after my mother died. My father took me into his home, but I never had a place there. I wanted to be with him because he was all I had, but he was a tremendous sexist. He expected great things from his sons and very little from me because I was a girl. My education wasn't as important as my looking pretty and he thought he was indulging me when he invested in my company. He doted on me when it suited him and Odessa hated me for it. From the time I was five, she told me I was stupid and ugly, an abomination, a mistake, a burden and an embarrassment. Later, when I grew curves, I was a harlot and a source of shame. *Like my mother.*" She flicked out a hand, batting away the countless other insults that had been hurled over the years.

"Now that my father is gone, and she has this excuse, Odessa isn't holding back," she continued. "She will do everything in her power to make me regret my own existence. She's more than capable of it. I have often wished I had never been born, but that doesn't matter because *I* don't matter, as she has made clear a thousand times."

"Ilona." Leander's breath hissed in and his hand came out.

She tucked her elbow into her side, going stiff with rejection.

"Think what you want of me, Leander. I don't care." That was mostly true. She didn't want to care what he thought of her. "Just tell me whether I should cancel our engagement party this weekend. I could use the time more productively elsewhere."

He was staring hard enough to scorch the side of her face, but she only watched Ursula happily chattering away out there, oblivious to the war going on in here.

In a sudden move, Leander knocked on the window to catch Ursula's attention.

"The party is on," he said darkly. "We'll marry here and find something else that suits us better as a home."

CHAPTER SIX

DO WHATEVER APPEASES that sickness inside you.

That serrated knife of a remark from Ilona stuck itself deep in Leander's gut and slowly turned.

You don't know what they put me through, he had wanted to rail at her, but maybe she did. Maybe she did.

It was a disturbing thought that kept closing his hands into fists, as though he was trying to catch hold of something he hadn't glimpsed long enough to identify before it was gone. His mind kept conjuring her stillness, her sadness beneath that cloak of dignity that had struck him as tattered and torn while she explained why she wouldn't risk asking him to raise a child who wasn't his.

It had sickened him to hear it. He hadn't wanted to believe her.

But he had. Midas, it seemed, had not fallen

far from the proverbial tree. His mother sounded equally sadistic and conscienceless.

So Leander was going ahead with this twisted alliance of theirs.

The rest of his week was nonstop meetings, allowing no time to see his fiancée. They mostly communicated through their assistants, much of it benign queries. Did he have opinions on wedding themes, menus or the font for the invitations? Leander did not. Did Ilona have a special request for their honeymoon? She did not.

The day of their engagement party arrived and it was one more appointment in today's packed calendar. Leander was on his way to his barber when Androu handed him an envelope marked Private and Confidential. The return address was Ilona Callas.

It jolted him to a halt in the middle of his office, but he didn't shy from whatever the envelope contained. He didn't know what he expected. A scathing suggestion he go forth and multiply? Perhaps the ring he'd given her?

It was a report from Ilona's physician certifying her pregnancy test was negative. She was also free of sexually transmitted infections and was deemed generally healthy, if slightly anemic. Her blood type was O positive.

Not pregnant. This was meant to satisfy any lingering doubts he might have, but it made him feel small. He swore tiredly.

"Kýrie?" Androu was hovering in anticipation of instructions.

"Book me an appointment with my doctor."

"Blood tests are only mandatory if you're marrying in a church. I looked it up."

"Book me an appointment, Androu."

"Immediately," Androu mumbled into his shirt front and exited the room.

A few hours later, Leander stopped by the clinic for the necessary procedures before making his way to his yacht.

Ilona was already aboard. On his instruction, she'd been given his stateroom for whatever entourage was helping her dress. He was already in his suit and found her in the shade of the lido deck, eating finger foods off a plate while listening intently to a young man who was gesturing as he spoke.

Leander's breath was punched out of him at the sheer beauty of her.

Her lightweight dress of ivory and seafoam

green was pressed to her curves by the breeze. Most of her gleaming black hair had been gathered into a professionally messy pile of curls, but wisps drifted around her face. The style would allow the wind to muss it without damaging the look, he imagined, but that hint of dishevelment was sensual and touchable. Playful and enticing.

The young man splashed something invisible onto his own face and Ilona burst into laughter, covering her mouth. Her profile was so bright and naturally joyous, her body language so relaxed and graceful, Leander had to catch his breath again.

"May I bring you a drink?" someone asked at his elbow, forcing him to drag his gaze from her.

"Scotch over ice," he said abstractly. When he looked back, Ilona had ironed her expression into an aloof mask. She offered him a cool smile.

"Leander. I don't think you've had a chance to meet Feodor in person." Ilona introduced the twentysomething who wore glasses and a goatee.

"It's a pleasure to meet you, Kýrie Vasilou,"

Feodor said with a respectful nod. He glanced at Ilona. "Shall I help with guest arrivals?"

"Thank you."

Feodor melted away and Leander watched him go with a hostile gladness he'd never experienced before. Was he really threatened by his fiancée's nerdy employee? How adolescent of him.

But the PA obviously knew Ilona very well. Well enough to make her laugh.

"Did he tell you a joke?" He hated himself for wanting to know.

"Hmm? Oh. No." Her expression softened. "His niece and nephew are characters. I enjoy hearing about them. This yacht is beautiful." She quickly changed the subject and set aside the plate she was holding. "I can see why you like to host parties here."

"I like it because it forces people to show up on time or miss departure. The sunset waits for no one. You look lovely."

"Thank you," she said automatically, as though she thought he was only saying what was expected and she was returning in kind. He meant it, though. He could hardly take his eyes off her.

"I got your report," he said, wondering if that would make her look at him.

"Good." She smiled at the server who brought his scotch and requested a glass of wine.

"I took all the same tests today," Leander informed her as the server moved out of earshot. "Most of the results will take a few days, but they were able to tell me right away that I'm not pregnant."

"Reassuring," she said without inflection, but her lips twitched. She glanced away to hide it.

The most ridiculous tickle of triumph spread through his chest.

They didn't have time for any more banter. Guests were arriving.

They had kept the party semiformal and small enough that it felt exclusive. "Small" was still a hundred guests. Once underway, Leander circulated with Ilona through the various saloons and outer decks, accepting congratulations and making small talk.

It would have been boring as hell, but he was fascinated, watching her navigate the different social connections. Her manners were impeccable and she was charming in a way that kept all the focus on their guests. She was incredibly good at deflecting while revealing very little about herself. It made him feel privileged to know that tiny bit more about her than she allowed anyone else to see, even though it was only a microscopic amount.

He reacted to her presence beside him, too. The crush of people had her standing close enough that her body heat radiated into his while the cobweb weight of her skirt fluttered against his pant leg. His ring glittered on her finger when she dragged a wisp of hair behind her ear and a caterer passed close enough behind them that Leander protectively set his hand on her lower back to ensure she didn't bump into the tray of drinks.

A soft pink flush touched her cheeks and her lashes lifted in question.

The noise fell away and the crackling awareness between them intensified. His hand was still on her back and his thumb moved in a restless caress. He had the nearly irresistible urge to draw her into an embrace.

"Ilona. I thought your family would be here." A middle-aged woman with zero sense of timing broke into their moment with an abrasive, "I was looking for Odessa."

There was a brief, hunted flash behind Ilona's eyes before she adopted her serene, welcoming expression.

"Leander, do you know Mira and Theodore? Mira lunches with my stepmother."

"Theodore and I are well acquainted," Leander said, shaking the husband's hand. It was clammy with sweat. "My mother couldn't make it, either," Leander added as an explanation for neglecting to invite anyone with the name Pagonis.

"I thought we had a scheduling conflict ourselves," Mira said through a pinched mouth. "But Theodore made it happen." That curled lip wasn't a smile.

"Wouldn't have missed it," Theodore assured Leander as he swept his handkerchief across his beaded forehead. "Congratulations to both of you. I'm sure you'll be very happy."

"I'm sure we will. And I'm glad we were able to clear up our own scheduling conflict with your project," Leander said magnanimously.

"Yes, yes. Excellent news." Theodore shot a warning glare at his wife as she made a sour noise.

"We're in demand tonight. Excuse us," Leander said.

"Enjoy your party," Theodore said behind them.

"She looks like she'd rather jump overboard," Ilona murmured as they moved away.

"She's welcome to," Leander retorted.

Ilona stifled a snort and shot a laughter-filled look up at him.

He bit back his own grin and set his hand on her waist again, liking the supple feel of her and the way all those feminine fragrances rose off her hair and skin to tantalize him.

"Let's see if we can find someone we can stand." He brought her to a business partner who had since become a friend, Mikolas, and his wife, Viveka. Viveka was an artist and very eager to tell Ilona how much she loved her products.

"Between painting and children, I'm washing up nonstop. I'd have hands like a scullery maid if not for your lotion. Have you thought of developing a children's line?"

They spoke with the couple until the champagne was served. The toasts were mostly bland platitudes, but Leander thanked every-

one for coming and set his arm around Ilona
as he lifted his glass to her.

"Finally, to my beautiful fiancée. By agreeing to marry me, you're giving me something
I've wanted for a long time." The words were
exactly as he'd rehearsed them, but they didn't
come out with near as much irony as he had
used to compose them.

The yacht must have hit some wash from
a passing freighter at that moment. The deck
seemed to shift beneath him as he watched her
drop her lashes. Shy at being the focus of attention? Or aware that he had intended to be
facetious and was stung by it?

"I mean it, *glykiá mou*." His voice sank into
his chest and he grew hot and prickly. "Thank
you."

Ilona didn't know what to make of Leander's
toast. Of any of this.

She had sent him that medical report in a
passive-aggressive huff, hurt and affronted.
The last thing she had expected—the very last
thing—was that he would make a joke about
taking a pregnancy test himself.

It had been such an absurd remark, she'd been

privately laughing about it all evening while re-
senting him for making it hard for her to hate
him. He was the loveliest date which was annoying, always nearby without smothering or
hovering. He checked on her drink and neither
monopolized a conversation nor left it all to
her. He knew how to get away from the boor-
ish guests, too.

And he'd gotten the upper hand with Odessa!
Ilona couldn't help enjoying what a ruthless
flex it was for him to neutralize Odessa's influence by pressuring Mira's husband into showing up, even if it meant the odious Mira was
here.

Ilona couldn't help admiring the strength
of his muscled frame, either, when the yacht
rocked beneath them and his arm firmed to
steady her. She honestly felt light-headed for
a moment and feared he was about to kiss her.
She would dissolve again; she really would and
couldn't bear to do it in front of all these people.

Thankfully, Feodor was keeping to his efficient schedule and the loud bang of fireworks
drew everyone outside.

The gasps and sighs of the crowd, the music

and the bursts of sparkling color, barely made an impression on Ilona. She stood with her back pressed to Leander's chest, her head resting in the hollow of his shoulder, her bottom brushing his hips and thighs. Her blood shot and fizzed with each shooting star then her heart exploded and her mind scattered.

It finally ended to great applause and the yacht pointed itself back to shore.

Leander's warm hands rubbed her cool arms. "Are you cold?"

"I brought warm clothes for nightfall. I'll go change."

She excused herself, skin still sensitized by a touch that surely wasn't meant to turn her on the way it did.

It was starting to hit her that this would be her life for the next three years. She would share a house with him and they would go to events and he would touch her shoulder to get her attention and her knees would go weak. How would she survive it?

The distress of her thoughts made her fingers clumsy. She couldn't seem to get these criss-cross laces to close her linen trousers and threw off her pullover, growing hot and agitated.

"Oh." Leander walked in and firmly pressed the door shut behind him.

"What—?" She snatched up the pullover and hugged it across her naked breasts, keeping her other hand on her unlaced pants so they wouldn't slide to the floor. "What are you doing here?"

"I thought you'd be finished changing. I need a clean shirt." He removed his jacket to reveal the stain of red wine on his chest.

"Did you lose a duel?"

"One of our guests had too much to drink." He began unbuttoning his shirt, gaze on the cuffs he was releasing. "If I were in a duel, I wouldn't lose."

"Says the man defeated by a glass of wine."

"Touché."

"Oof. I see what you did there. You should be ashamed of yourself."

"Yet I rarely am," he said in a blithe tone while stepping into the closet.

She seized the opportunity to shrug on her pullover again. It had a wide neckline that didn't allow for a bra. Its loose sleeves and drawstring cuffs got in the way as she hurried to work on the cords of her trouser fly. Why was looking chic always so inconvenient?

She finally managed it and set her bare foot on the bed so she could turn her pants cuff. She used her comb to measure the width, ensuring they were exactly the same.

"You don't have to try so hard, you know." He spoke from the door of the closet and his voice had shifted to a lower gear. He was closing the cuffs on a clean shirt that hung open, revealing his bare torso. He belonged on a romance novel cover, he was so muscled and well proportioned. She swallowed, gaze fixated on that intriguing pattern of chest hair that bisected his six-pack then disappeared into his boxers as he opened his fly and tucked his shirt.

That knocked her out of her staring. Nervously, she stepped in front of the full-length mirror and smoothed the hint of a wrinkle near her pocket, then adjusted the fall of the pullover on her bare shoulders.

"This necklace doesn't work with this collar, does it?" Its square links had contrasted appealingly with the sweetheart neckline of her sundress, but they were too heavy a statement for the soft, bohemian knit.

She searched with her fingertips for the catch behind her neck.

"Did you hear me?" Leander appeared behind her in the mirror, a loose tie slung beneath his popped collar. His warm fingers brushed hers aside and worked the catch on her necklace. His breath stirred the fine hairs at the base of her skull, sending a shiver down her spine.

As he brought his hand in front of her, offering the necklace, his smoky gaze met hers in the mirror. "You're beautiful. That's not false flattery. I'm being completely honest."

"That's nice of you to say, but Odessa's friends will make a full report." She accepted the necklace. "They'll buy themselves back into her good graces by disparaging me for any little infraction they can find."

He made a dismissive noise, but his dark brows came together as his attention went to the spot where her shoulder met her neck.

"You have something here— A birthmark?" His thumb rubbed where she'd had laser treatments until it was only a slight discoloration. "Is it a scar?"

"Is it unsightly?" The question was a deflection. She didn't want to admit Midas had once pushed Hercules on the swing hard enough to hit her and knock her down, leaving a cut that would have concussed her if it had been on her scalp. "I should have brought something else to wear. I can take my hair down to hide it."

"No, I only noticed because I'm standing right here…" His thumb was still brushing over the scar, sending little tingles into her breasts. "Is it the result of a hot curler mishap? I'm serious. Don't hurt yourself trying to improve on perfection." His gaze flickered to hers in the mirror, gently admonishing, but filled with the warmth of masculine admiration.

"You really are laying it on thick," she chided, trying not to melt under that look.

To her eternal shock, he dipped his head and pressed a warm kiss against the old injury.

Her nipples blossomed with a sting beneath the sensual knit and she drew in a shaken breath.

His gaze came up. "No?"

"I—" She didn't know. Except she did. Because his hand flexed at her waist and her eyes were growing hot and damp. She had become one live wire of pulsing sensation. Her whole body, which had been tracking him at a subconscious level all evening, was now fully awake and aching for his touch.

All from one innocent kiss.

Was it innocent, though? He knew what he was doing. His gaze was hazed with lust as he watched her.

"Tell me what you're thinking," he coaxed.

It was embarrassing and far too revealing, but try as she might, she couldn't look away or dissemble. Not right now. Not with him.

She bit her lips together, helpless against the reaction that was taking her over.

His breath dragged in and his eyelids grew heavier.

"I'm dying to know if this scent on you is the result of all your lotions or if it's just the way you smell." His nose and lips brushed her nape, barely grazing her skin, but the caress made her scalp tighten and a soft moan climbed in her throat. "It's intoxicating." His hot breath pooled against the side of her throat. "You have to tell me, Ilona. Do you want me to kiss you? Touch you?"

"Yes," she whispered. Whimpered. Her assent slid from her lips before she could think better of it.

"Good." The low word seemed to emanate from the depths of his chest. He opened his mouth more deliberately against her skin. Her whole body went weak.

His arms came around her, one hand sliding under the edge of her pullover, splaying across her bare abdomen as he dragged her into the strength of his frame.

"This is what I wanted to do to you when we were outside. Could you feel how much I want you?"

She opened her mouth, but no sound came out. She was too inundated by wild sensations. He wasn't even doing anything except setting those soft kisses under her ear and lightly kneading her belly, but she grew shakier by the second. She could feel his heart hitting her shoulder blade, heavy and strong, and there was a pressure against her bottom that should have intimidated her, but it thrilled her. She was affecting him, too.

She didn't know what to do with her hands except to cup his jaw and turn her face, seeking his mouth with her own.

With a groan, he dragged her even closer. His hot mouth stole over hers and instantly she was drowning. She didn't care. This was the primitive jungle of that night at dinner. A place where she didn't even feel self-conscious when his hand found its way up beneath her shirt to cup her braless breast. She could only tremble in reaction and let her mouth part wider so he could kiss her more deeply.

He turned her and sandwiched her against the cold, smooth wall of the mirror with the warm press of his body. Both his hands came up beneath her pullover to possess her breasts while his mouth plundered hers.

She hadn't known any kiss could feel like this. Like a drug. Like a craving. She swept her hands up and down his sides and around to his back, tracing the indent of his spine and urging him to crush her because his weight felt so good against her.

"This is all I think about," he growled against her cheek, thumbs circling and circling her distended nipples, sending runnels of heat and need deep into her loins.

His knee barely suggested inserting itself between hers and she flowered open, accepting his hard thigh against her mound with a shaken gasp of gratitude.

While the edge of his teeth stole down her neck and he sucked on her earlobe and swept his tickling caress across her breasts, all her focus drilled down to the bright, hot place where his hard thigh pinned itself to her pulsing flesh.

She was moving against him, she realized. Seeking those sharp, piercing bolts of pleasure. She was as shameless as she was mindless. Her hands were clenched in his hair and she was arching and shifting, needing that hard pressure, needing everything he could give her. She returned his kiss with flagrant passion, sucking on his bottom lip, asking him for something. *More.*

He muttered something about never lasting three years and loosened her laced fly. The wide strength of his palm went into her pants and covered the lace underwear she wore, hot and sure.

"Yes? Tell me yes." It was both a command and a plea. His eyes sparked stardust from behind the filter of his spiky lashes. His knowing touch stole beneath the silk and—

"Oh." Lightning struck as he caressed that

spot, that sweet, taut, needy spot. Again and again.

"Say it," he urged, rubbing and circling.

"Yes," she panted helplessly. "Yes. Don't stop. Oh, Leander. Oh, oh—" She was on her tiptoes, seeking. *Needing* the invasion of his finger. Needing the rocking of his palm that utterly owned her.

"Now, *glykiá mou.*" His mouth covered hers and the oblivion swept up in a shivering wave, taking her out of herself for long moments where she was only dimly aware of how uninhibited she was as her body pulsated in ecstasy.

CHAPTER SEVEN

"WE'LL STAY ABOARD TONIGHT." Leander's thick voice dragged her back to herself. His gaze was smoldering as he eased his hand from between them.

Ilona was still trembling and so embarrassed, she wished she would die of it. Please. Right now. An iceberg. *Anything.*

He was holding her up because she was still clinging to him. Had she really let him touch her like that? And make her orgasm while he was fully dressed and in complete control of his own body? He was aroused, yes. The press of his erection against her was unmistakable, but he wasn't panting and melted and falling apart the way she just had.

"Unless you want to forget about saying good-night to our guests? I could definitely be talked into not leaving this room for the rest of the week." His teeth were at her earlobe again, letting her feel the scrape of them.

Even as her hair seemed to stand on end with renewed stimulation, she knew she couldn't sleep with him. For a multitude of reasons, not least of which was the fact he had the power to make her forget every one of those reasons.

With an inner cringe, she realized people would be noting their absence and their change of attire when they reappeared. Rumors would get back to Odessa that something had happened in here and that could turn ugly very fast.

"I'll go out first," she decided, opening the hands that were clenched in his shirt and pressing him back.

"Good idea. I need a minute," he said wryly before catching her lips in a final, pulse-fluttering kiss that had her mouth clinging so helplessly to his.

He closed himself into the bathroom, but she stayed exactly where she was, still too shaken to move. Too mortified. *Scared.*

For all those rumors Odessa had circulated about how promiscuous Ilona was, she was actually a virgin. Sex meant babies and, much as she yearned for a family, she knew how vulnerable children made a woman. She didn't remember much about her mother, but she remembered her counting out money and crying. She remembered her watching Ilona eat without placing a plate in front of herself.

And that was without someone actively trying to destroy her because she had dared to have a child.

She couldn't stay the night with Leander! She wasn't on the pill or anything.

Pushing off the mirror, she turned to confront herself and, even though he had just rewritten everything she had believed about her sexual self, she looked remarkably untouched. Her trousers needed retying, but they were barely wrinkled. Her nipples were still tender, but they were relaxed beneath the soft knit. Her makeup was unsmudged and she only had to reapply the lipstick that had faded through the evening.

Her hand wasn't quite steady, but she managed it. Then she sat to fasten her wedge heels with their ribbon ties.

She wasn't fast enough. Leander emerged as she was rising. She turned to give herself a final inspection, mostly to avoid his gaze.

"People are going to think what they think,

Ilona. Screw them." He held out a hand. "Let's finish this so I can have you to myself."

She didn't tell him she would leave as planned, thinking it was better to wait until they'd both cooled off.

Despite her intense self-consciousness and latent tension, the rest of the evening was pleasant, if disconcerting. Each time her arm brushed Leander's or he glanced toward her, a spike of renewed desire shot through her, shutting down her brain and amping her nerve endings back to life.

Finally, the guests were filing off the yacht, all professing the party a wonderful night.

Then Mira proved herself to be the drunk who had ruined Leander's shirt. She lurched out of her husband's arm and jabbed her sharp fingernail into Ilona's breastbone.

"She knows what you're doing," she slurred. "You think you can cash in with a baby? She won't allow it. She told me she won't."

Theodore muttered an imprecation and firmly steered Mira off the yacht while the handful of remaining guests pretended nothing had happened.

Ilona could feel the demand for answers radiating off Leander's stiff presence, though.

As the last guest departed, Feodor approached. "I think that went well. I'll see you Monday?"

"I'm coming back with you," Ilona said, swallowing the nervous quaver that arrived in her voice. "Would you mind fetching my things?" She didn't look at Leander.

"Of cour—"

"I'll take you in my car," Leander told her. "Feodor can drop Androu."

Feodor bounced his surprised gaze to Leander then back to Ilona. As the silence drew out, he said, "I'll fetch your bag," adeptly solving half the problem and leaving them to work out the rest.

"I'll have the cars brought around." Androu hurried away in the opposite direction.

Moments later, Ilona was settling into the shadowed interior of Leander's car. He told Dino to "check the score" and waited for the man to put in his earbuds before saying in a dangerous tone, "Care to explain what *cash in with a baby* means?"

Not especially. She rolled her lips inward as she considered how much to say, but he was likely to find out once he was voting her shares at Pagonis anyway.

"There's a provision in my father's will to reapportion the family shares when babies are born."

There was a stunned silence, then, "Spell it out for me. Are you saying that if I get you pregnant, our child will eat up shares that belong to the rest of the family?"

"Yes."

"Why haven't you told me that?"

"Because I don't wish to be used as a brood mare or have my child used as a property stake."

"That's not what I'm suggesting."

"Tell me that's not the first thought that popped into your mind," she scoffed.

His cheek ticked and he looked away. "I've trained myself to look at every option with an objective lens, especially when it comes to taking your brother down. That doesn't mean I would follow through on something so cold-blooded. Midas would, though. Why hasn't he?"

Ilona bit back a sigh, finding this whole topic distasteful. "He tried as soon as he married.

That was seven years ago, but they didn't have any luck. Apparently, he had gonorrhea when he was at uni and left it untreated for years. Four years ago, after his divorce, he supposedly got another woman pregnant, but our father was still alive. He insisted on a paternity test. The baby wasn't Midas's. Our father wrote in a condition that the family shares can only be held by Pagonis blood."

"That all tracks," Leander said with a disgusted snort. "What about the other one?"

"Hercules? He isn't interested in women or children."

"So that leaves you. If *you* carry a baby, it's definitely a Pagonis. No wonder they're so threatened by you."

"Yes, and everything they put me through would be visited upon my child tenfold so I *can't*."

"I would protect both of you. You have to know that."

"I would love to believe it," she assured him. "But why do *you* suddenly want a baby? I was raised on spite, Leander. I refuse to conceive a baby simply to get the better of them. Kindly don't ask me to."

"I'm not." He didn't flinch. "But you do want children. Don't you?" It wasn't really a question. He was prodding for confirmation.

She did. Deep down, she had a flicker of a dream where her life was filled with love. Where high small voices said the words to her and a deep one said it across a pillow and she even said it herself. And meant it. She wanted it to spill out of her in the most sincere and healing way, making her feel worthy and needed. Whole.

She didn't tell him any of that, only left a thick silence that had him turning his face to the window.

They didn't speak again until they were at her building. As he got out to hold the door and assist her, he said, "We'll talk more about this tomorrow."

"No we won't," she muttered and went inside.

Why do you *want a baby?*

Children hadn't been at the top of his immediate list of goals; Leander would admit that. Conceiving an heir was something he had firmly placed on the back burner while he spent all his concentration and effort on righting the wrong Midas had done to him.

He had always assumed he would have children at some point, though. His relationship with his mother was strained, but he had been close with his father. Maybe there was even a sense of something left undone. He had lost his father when he was sixteen. It was a time of life when many an adolescent walked out on their parents, determined to mature on their own terms.

Leander hadn't had the luxury of choice and often wondered what his father would think of the person he had become. Would he be this jaded, driven man if his father hadn't died? Would his father appreciate what Leander was trying to do in his memory? Was there any sense in doing it if he wasn't going to pass his name and legacy on to another generation of Vasilous?

So yes, he wanted children for deeply personal reasons that had nothing to do with any advantage they might afford him with his mission against Midas Pagonis.

Obviously, he wouldn't force any woman to carry his child if she didn't want to, but given the security he could offer, he had been a little insulted that first day when Ilona had said, *I don't want children with* you, summarily rejecting him as if he failed to measure up.

There were extenuating circumstances; he saw that now, and he understood her suspicion of his motives, but he was the product of an accidental pregnancy. He wouldn't be cavalier about bringing children into anything but a committed, healthy relationship.

Which was *not* what they had.

They *did* have incredible chemistry, though. If they hadn't had guests to get back to, they very well might have risked a pregnancy while they'd been aboard the yacht. That encounter had been erotic and exciting and Leander had suddenly seen their three-year stretch of marriage as something that would be the furthest thing from celibate.

He wasn't taking anything for granted, but if they had sex, a baby became possible. For that reason, they had to discuss how they would handle pregnancy and children.

Over the next two days, he tried to reach Ilona to hash it out, but she put him off, canceling a dinner date and claiming she had too many things going on at work.

Annoyed, he instructed his lawyer to add baby bonuses and other settlements to their agreement.

Ilona's response came through her own lawyer. She accepted his terms as a contingency, but she expected him to abide by their "gentleman's agreement" regarding separate bedrooms. Also, she had a dress fitting and couldn't make lunch.

So childish.

Her silent treatment continued as he was called to Rome. Midas was being a nuisance, interfering with a project there, but Leander quickly got it back on track.

He returned two days later to a text that Ilona didn't need to view the property his agent had found. If he liked it, he could proceed with the purchase.

Was this what their marriage would be like? Hot and cold? He could have accepted that more easily if he wasn't still tantalized by the knowledge that when it was hot, it was *very* hot.

He would have to be the adult and reach out yet again, he supposed, but he had just arrived home and wanted to work off his tension. He changed into his gym clothes and started on the treadmill, watching financial headlines while he ran.

He was so deep in thought, he nearly missed a call that jammed his otherwise healthy heart.

Ilona knew Leander was back in Athens, but he didn't call or text.

That shouldn't bother her. They weren't teenagers where every text or lack thereof held a dozen hidden meanings.

She hadn't meant for their discussion on children to turn into such a bone of contention, but the way Mira had brought it up on the heels of their intimacy had made Ilona very defensive.

For the first time in her life, the idea of having sex was very enticing, but she wanted Leander to want *her*, not an incubator for another figurine on his chessboard. When the email had come through from the lawyers, listing all the benefits—bribes?—he'd offered if she became pregnant, she'd felt pressured and struck back with firm boundaries.

Even though she wanted sex with him. She couldn't lie to herself about that.

As for having a baby, well, it was a huge step, but she and Leander were both very wealthy, not counting pennies the way her mother had been. Pregnancy and child-rearing wouldn't be a hardship, not the way it was for some who had much less.

As for the danger of Midas and Odessa coming after her child, Leander *would* do everything in his power to protect what was his. She believed that.

No, now that she'd had time to think calmly about it, she wasn't as adamant against the idea of children, but she still saw issues in having a baby with a man who, at best, felt ambivalent about her. Eventually that lack of a bond between them would either force them to stay in a loveless arrangement for the sake of their child, or part and bring stepparents into the equation.

Neither of those outcomes appealed to her.

Amid her ruminations, her door buzzed.

Probably her neighbor Rasmus. His cat was forever leaping from his fire escape onto the outside ledge, then walking around to cry at the windows of the other units on this floor. Rasmus left his door unlocked so residents could return Snuggles, but Ilona often kept him if she was having a night in.

She'd been about to step into the bath, but she tightened the belt on her robe and hurried to tell him Snuggles wasn't here. She glanced through the peephole and saw flowers.

Leander? Her heart softened like butter in the sun.

She swung the door open, a smile dawning on her face because there was no reason to suspect it would be *Midas*.

CHAPTER EIGHT

LEANDER IDENTIFIED HIMSELF as Ilona's fiancé and the flustered building manager took him up to her floor.

"We're still investigating how the intruder was allowed up," the manager said in the elevator. "We have protocols around announcing visitors, but a new employee was in today."

Convenient.

"He was only here a minute or two. Security came up immediately, but he was already gone down the fire stairs."

"Have you reported it to the police?"

"Kyría Callas asked that they not be involved."

"Involve them." The doors opened and Leander stepped into a hallway where someone with a security badge snapped to attention. A resident shrank into their flat and closed the door.

One door stood open. Roses were spilled like bloodstains across the hardwood. Leander could see a lamp was overturned and a floor rug askew.

A grotesque premonition came over him. An echo of the day he'd found his father. He swallowed, stomach sour and skin turning clammy as he approached.

"Ilona," he called out, voice thick and unsteady.

"She's in there," the security guard said, pointing to a closed door.

Leander knocked. "Ilona, it's me. Let me in."

There was a pause, then firm footsteps approached. A man of his own age let him in.

A whirling tornado of emotions pushed him inside. A dozen questions were on his tongue. *Why did you call Feodor, not me? Why did you let Midas in? Why don't you want the police involved?*

He wanted answers and—

He froze, unable to breathe.

Midas had only been here a minute or two, but she looked…broken. She wasn't crying, but her eyes were swollen and her face ravaged by tear tracks. There was a bin of crumpled tissues beside the sofa and a box of fresh ones on the coffee table. The light that usually radiated off her was nearly winked out. Her shoulders were hunched, her legs covered with a soft yellow blanket. Her hands were protectively folded over a tortoiseshell cat.

As he approached, her eyes swallowed her face and her mouth trembled. What kicked him in the stomach hardest was the glint of embarrassment in her eyes. She hated that he was seeing her like this.

"You said Feodor was coming." She darted a look to the man who had let him in.

"I…" The man shrugged. "When he called back, he said to tell you he was coming. I didn't know he meant someone else."

"He shouldn't have called you," she said to Leander. "I'm fine. I just need a minute." She dabbled a tissue into the corner of her eye and took a big breath, trying to rally herself.

The air in his lungs turned hot. *Don't*, he wanted to say. He wanted to squeeze her hand and gather her up and whisper that everything would be okay now, but she looked so brittle, he was afraid she would disintegrate if he touched her.

He wanted to know what Midas had said to scare the hell out of her like this.

"Androu was with Feodor," Leander said absently. "He called me when he realized what was going on." Leander suspected the pair had been in bed. What his employee did in his off time was none of his business unless there was a possibility of professional compromise. In this case, it had definitely worked to his advantage. "I told Feodor I would take care of everything."

"Can I get you coffee? Tea?" a woman asked.

"No. I'm taking Ilona home."

"I don't want to go in there." Ilona's voice was a whisper-thin husk of its usually sensual self, thick with a plea not to make her face it.

"I'll take you to *my* home. You'll be safe there." He crouched beside her. "Do you want me to go pack your bag for you?"

"Would you?" She seemed anxious, as though it was the biggest ask in the world to walk across the hall. "There's one in the closet that I keep packed for travel. And my phone. It's on the charger. And my purse? I know I'm being a coward, but..." She bit her quivering lips and looked to the ceiling, trying to catch back the fresh tears that were welling.

That's when he saw the red marks on her throat. They nearly knocked him on his ass.

Blackout rage might have taken him then, but the woman said, "You need clothes to wear in the car. Do you want me to find something? Then I can help you dress?"

Ilona nodded.

Leander stood and took advantage of the moment to step away from Ilona and get hold of himself. He could hardly breathe, he was so explosive with fury. He went across to her flat and into her bathroom where he emptied the tepid tub. Then he splashed cold water on his face and the back of his neck, trying to cool his temper enough to behave like a civilized human being.

Trying to quiet the voice that said, *Kill him*.

The neighbor woman was gone when he came out. He looked around Ilona's apartment. It was small, only one bedroom, but it was nicely laid out and welcoming. He liked the warm tones and lack of clutter and comfortable textures. It smelled like her.

It was clearly her safe space, but she no longer felt safe here. That infuriated him all over again. He cleaned up the flowers and glass, then found her bag. He had security take it down with some fresh dry cleaning and her laptop. He threw all the medications he could find into her handbag along with her phone and the keys from a bowl by the door.

When he came to collect her, Ilona was dressed in matching track pants and jacket, bare feet tucked into a pair of sandals. Her face was washed, her hair combed and gathered in a ponytail. She was still sallow, but the shaken vulnerability of twenty minutes ago was firmly packed away behind a mask of polite gratitude.

"You've been very kind," she said to the couple. "I'm sorry I interrupted your evening."

They reassured her it was no trouble and Leander nodded his own thanks before he escorted Ilona into the elevator. There was a robotic quality to her body language. Her gaze was unblinking, her expression blank, her movements seeming to be on autopilot.

He wasn't much better, but his jerky sightlessness was the result of the tight control he was using to suppress his bloodthirsty wrath. She needed reassurance, not an exhibition of further male aggression, but that aggression was there and it would emerge when the time was right. Midas would definitely pay for this.

"You drove yourself?" Ilona was briefly confounded when Leander opened the passenger door of a green-and-silver convertible.

"Dino was already home for the evening." Leander placed a call as he started the car.

"Androu," his assistant answered.

"Order curbside. Chicken for two."

That confused her, too. She wasn't hungry and time had ceased to move while she had sat on her neighbor's sofa.

Thank goodness her neighbor, Rasmus, had left his door unlocked. Midas had attacked her, but her self-defense training had kicked in just as quickly. She had dropped him with a knee to the groin, then barged into the apartment next door, before locking Midas in the hall to shout profanities. His voice had faded even as Rasmus was calling security. Ilona suspected Rasmus had been making love with that woman, but Ilona had stayed there anyway, ruining their evening, too afraid to go into her own home.

That's why she was in Leander's car, valiantly trying to work out what she ought to do next, but her brain simply refused to work. She could hardly make sense of simple things like why there was so much traffic when it felt like the middle of the night. When had she opened her door to Midas? An hour ago?

"Is Kyría Callas with you?" Androu's disembodied voice was asking. "Feodor has dispatched bodyguards to escort her—"

"She's with me. I'm taking her home."

"Ilona?" Feodor's voice came through the speaker. "I've initiated red-level security at the Callas building and amber levels at all the international facilities. I have a secure location for you to stay in. Where should Eugene collect you? What else do you need? Clothes? Personal products? Are you hurt?"

"I'm fine," she said, more baffled than ever. "Why are you with Androu?"

"She's not fine," Leander cut in. "Have her doctor come to my apartment." Leander poked to end the call. "They're seeing one another."

"Feodor and Androu?" Her brain was still stumbling over his doctor edict. "Since when?"

"Since they went home together off the yacht, I imagine."

"Oh. That's nice for them. Is Androu nice?

Feodor deserves someone nice." He was more than her PA. He was her best friend. Her only friend and she paid him very well to be as trustworthy and accessible as he was. She had had to use Rasmus's phone to call him so he hadn't picked up the unknown number, but he had listened to her voice mail straightaway. He had dealt with everything while she had sat on Rasmus's sofa, numb, incapable of helping herself.

"Androu is smart, efficient and loyal enough to call *me* when you were in trouble. Why didn't you?"

"It didn't occur to me." She slouched deeper into her seat. "Feodor knows what to do. Don't be angry."

"I'm not angry at you. I'm angry at Midas and myself for not seeing how truly dangerous he is. Has he assaulted you before? Is that why you have all these security protocols that can be activated with a word?"

"Not recently." There had been that incident at the funeral, the one that had left her arm in a sling. Odessa had witnessed it and pretended she hadn't, but Feodor had talked Ilona into making a report to the police—which Leander would probably insist on as well. She headed that off by saying, "Look, I know I should make statements and everything, but it's *hard*. And nothing will happen. I can tell you right now Odessa will provide him with an alibi. She always does."

"Even when your father was alive?" He didn't raise his voice, but the simmering fury that imbued his tone thickened the air in the car. "Did *he* know Midas was violent?"

She turned her face to the window. "He put a stop to the worst of it."

A profound silence, then a grim, "But not all of it."

No. There had still been the pinches and shoves and her father hadn't had the patience for tattling so she had learned to keep her distance and her guard up.

"I know you think you can use this against him." Her voice cracked and she wanted to bury her face in her hands at the thought. "But I don't want to be your hammer, Leander. I just want to get away from him."

"You are away. I'm taking you away," he said firmly. "But this isn't about my desire for revenge, Ilona. He *hurt* you. That can't happen again. Together we'll make sure it doesn't."

She looked across at him, mouth trembling at how badly she wanted to believe him, but why would he help her? He didn't care about her, not really. Only as much as he cared about gaining access to an easy door to get to Midas.

"Can we not talk about it right now?" She was trying not to cry. "I don't want to think of it."

Leander couldn't stop thinking of it. He was incensed and gripped by the urgency to annihilate Midas, but he needed to know Ilona was safe, that she *felt* safe.

"You have the whole floor?" she asked when they stepped off his private elevator into his penthouse.

"One of the perks of building the building. I set this aside for myself." It had three bedrooms, but one was his office. The other was his personal gym. He hadn't thought of that when he'd brought her here, only that it was a suitable fortress. He had wanted to bring her into the place where he could protect her best.

He showed her the alarm panel and gave her a code to come and go, then explained the emergency system and how an alarm would sound and security would descend if anyone tried to override it. She seemed to relax a fraction as she took it all in.

While he plated their food, Ilona drifted through the living area like a ghost, pale and lifeless, pausing to admire his view of the Acropolis, his pool and the dining area that opened to a terrace that offered sunset views. His decor was an ultramodern style of clean lines and practicality. He wasn't one for pillows with froufrou tassels or colorful throw rugs like he'd seen at her place and he regretted that choice now. He would have liked to offer her those softer touches so she would feel more at ease.

Neither of them ate much and her physician arrived while they were still picking at their meals. She took Ilona into his bedroom to examine her. The doctor didn't say much as she left, only that Ilona had gone into the shower and would take a sedative and go to bed when she came out.

Leander made some calls, learning the cameras in Ilona's building had been disabled, the doorman who had let Midas up couldn't be located and Midas had been with his stepmother all evening—exactly as Ilona had predicted.

Leander swore under his breath, but he wasn't the least bit surprised. These sorts of dirty tactics were familiar to him from his own attempts to seek justice against the man. That's why he'd had to attack Midas through the unprotected flank of Ilona's company.

His desire to obliterate the man had increased a thousandfold, but he could no longer use Ilona to do it. His gut churned with guilt at having set her up for this attack. She might not have come right out and told him she was afraid Midas would assault her, but all the signs had been there. Leander had been too blinded by his thirst for vengeance to see it.

He had seen Ilona as Midas's weakness, but now she was his own Achilles' heel. Any further strikes Midas aimed at her would impact Leander. His conscience couldn't abide it and there was also something deeper. He'd tasted her fear and felt her shaken anguish inside his own chest. He hurt because she hurt.

It had been a long time since Leander had felt this vulnerable. He cared about people, but only collectively and superficially. He ensured appropriate policies were put in place for work-place conduct and safety. He paid livable wages and "gave back" and his company was founded on green principles.

But after the devastation of losing his father, he'd been careful not to become too emotionally attached to anyone. The worst he'd felt since then was when his PA had abruptly left with pregnancy complications. He'd hired Androu to replace her in a very sexist attempt not to experience such acute concern for an employee again.

In fact, one of the attractions of proposing to Ilona had been his initial antipathy toward her. He had been convinced he wouldn't come to care for her. Not in a way that would leave him open to being hurt. Yet here he was, knocking softly then slipping into his bedroom to stand over her sleeping form, ensuring she hadn't fallen in the shower and was resting comfortably.

She had aligned herself on the edge of the mattress, blankets pulled over her ear, hair woven into a shiny black tail he wanted to touch.

How arrogant of him to assume he could

bring a woman into his life and not bear any responsibility for what happened to her. The scope of that responsibility, one that encompassed the bruises on her throat, was deep enough to make his torso ache.

He didn't want this responsibility, this weight, but he definitely wanted Midas to pay. It was a dilemma that had him circling the bed and sitting down on the far side to consider his next moves.

There was no going backward on his plan to marry her. If anything, he had to double down and make it clear they were a team that Midas couldn't break. That meant they would have to begin to really trust one another.

It was still eating at him that she hadn't thought to call him and had been so shocked that he had turned up. His ego was more than dented over that. He felt genuine shame because why would she think of him as an ally when he was the reason Midas had come after her?

They needed to build a bridge between them, one that spanned a deep, jagged distance of familial betrayal and painful history. Bridges were his specialty in real life, but earning her trust and proffering his own was a much trickier project. It wouldn't be accomplished through a few exercises in eye contact and backward falls. They would have to genuinely open up and be honest with each other. It would take time and commitment.

It would mean completely letting his guard down with a Pagonis.

All his instincts knotted into a tangled shield at the very idea, but it was the only way to best Midas. He knew that.

He dropped onto his back beside her, considering how to go about it.

Ilona woke thirsty and disoriented. Weak morning light was coming through the crack in the curtains. Where—?

Memory rushed back. She was in Leander's home. His bed!

With a small gasp, she sat up, head swimming.

"You're safe, Ilona." Leander's voice was a quiet rumble beside her. "Go back to sleep."

He was still dressed in last night's clothes. Part of the bedspread was pulled across his waist. He had one arm thrown above his head, his eyes were closed and stubble shadowed his jaw.

Had he said the same thing in the night? She had a vague memory of waking with a whimper and hearing his reassuring voice beside her. He might have held her hand...

"I need to go to work," she said, reflexively looking for escape.

"Why?" Leander cracked one eye. "We can work from here."

"I want to go in." It was what she did. Carry on. Pretend it hadn't happened. Do the things she could control so she wouldn't dwell on things she couldn't.

She pulled up her knees and hugged them, considering whether that was the healthiest way to keep responding to Midas, especially if he was escalating from insulting and antagonizing to physical assaults.

As she closed her hot eyes and pressed them to her kneecaps, she started to relive that horrible moment when she had opened her door and—

Her hair shifted, sending a tingle across her scalp. A shiver went down her spine that made her lift her head and sit up straighter. That caused a light tug on her plait.

"I couldn't help myself," Leander said wryly as he released her thick tail so its weight landed against her back again. "It looks like it's carved from obsidian, it's so glossy and smooth."

She self-consciously brought the plait to the front of her shoulder and petted it, liking the silky, ropey feel of it herself.

"Feodor has made arrangements for me. I don't want to intrude on you longer tha—"

"Ilona." He came up on an elbow. "We're going to live together in ten days anyway. Stay here until then."

"Here?" She was striving for a cynical reference to the bed they were currently occupying, but she wasn't as averse to sharing it with him as she should be. Her stomach was tilting all over the place at the daunting yet alluring thought.

He inhaled sharply and caught the hand she was sweeping down the rippled line of her plait. Her pajama sleeve had fallen back, revealing the black bruise on her forearm.

"That—I hit it on something when I was..."

She tugged free and drew her sleeve to cover her wrist.

"When you were running away." His voice had turned bludgeon-hard again. "I want you to stay here, Ilona. Go into work each day if you must. I'll take you there myself, but he's not getting near you again. Not without going through me."

She didn't know how to react to that. It had been a long time since someone had been on her side. Feodor was, but he wasn't in a position to offer real protection. On the contrary, she protected him and the rest of her employees, taking whatever Midas dished out so they were shielded from it.

The pattern in the bedspread blurred. She couldn't look at Leander, she was so touched. He had come to her when she'd been too shocked to look after herself. He had said he was taking her away from them, that he wanted to *help* her. To guard her when she was so tired of guarding herself.

She had to bite her lips to still their trembling.

"Ilona?"

"Shall I make the coffee?" She threw back the covers and escaped before she broke down and threw herself at him.

CHAPTER NINE

ONCE LEANDER WAS SATISFIED that the security precautions in her work building were top-notch, he left her there for the day which helped settle her nerves. Work was Ilona's safe place. Her happy place. Here she made things that helped people and was liked and successful and valued.

Before she knew it, the day was gone and Leander had returned for her, which surprised her.

"You didn't have to come. I have body-guards." They'd been relegated to following in her car behind them since Leander had escorted her into his own. "I was planning to work late and get ahead on a few things before the wedding." Mostly she had wanted to put off facing him again along with all the changes that were happening so fast. Before last night, she had been counting on these final days of singlehood to come to terms with everything.

"I want to start dating," he said.

"Other people?" She was floored.

"Each other," he clarified dryly, mouth twitching.

"Oh." Her cheeks abruptly stung with a blush, as though she was an adolescent and he was the first boy to ask her to dance. "Why? We're already engaged. Living together." Kind of. Her things were being boxed from her apartment in preparation for their moving into the home they would share after their honeymoon. "I have a ton of things to do." She was restructuring at work and had fittings and decor decisions, not to mention signing her statement with the police and finishing up negotiations on their prenuptial contract.

"We need to get to know one another better."

In what way? Spend the night on his yacht sort of way?

The heat in her cheeks intensified.

Things had changed so much since that interlude at their engagement party. She'd been embarrassed by her response that night, then conflicted over Leander wanting to discuss children.

She still had huge reservations about making a baby with someone she didn't love, but she wanted a family. And she was so *tired* of being afraid to go after what she wanted. She was tired of trying to live up to impossible expectations set by people who didn't care about her.

Agreeing to marry Leander had been an act of defiance, one where she had finally seized control of her own life. Deciding her future, choosing what happened to her body and whether she had a family, should be her choice, too, not something dictated by whether Midas and Odessa would approve.

Since last night's attack, she had been considering more about that. She kept thinking that having a baby would be more than a rejection of Midas's control over her. It would be a defiance against her own mortality. Life was fragile and temporary. She had to get on with living the one she'd been given.

And there was that other, secretive defiance within her, the one where she *felt* things. Where she had discovered a sensuality she hadn't known she was capable of experiencing. Did she want to spend the next three years ignoring that? Then explore it with someone else?

Or did she want Leander to show her everything her body could feel?

"That wasn't a euphemism." Leander briefly squeezed her fingers where her hand rested on the seat between them, sending a zing up her arm and into her chest.

"Pardon?"

"I realize Midas has made it hard for you to trust any man. I'm not referring to sex. We need to know we can count on each other. That means spending time together. We need to be honest and work through any fears or disagreements we might have."

"You're afraid of me?" she asked skeptically.

"I'm afraid *for* you," he said gravely. "I'm bothered that you're afraid of me."

Was she? Not in the way he meant. She'd been sedated last night and even though he had shared the bed, the most intrusive thing he'd done was tell her to go back to sleep. She had awakened surprised, but not frightened.

Which was strange. The idea of sleeping next to someone had never appealed. Sleep was a very vulnerable state. She'd been taught that every weakness could be exploited, but waking next to Leander had been almost reassuring.

It was something she could easily get used to. Which was disturbing.

"I'm not afraid of you. I'm afraid to trust you," she clarified haltingly. "Finding my way to being as self-reliant as I am was hard. I try not to count on anyone. That way they can't disappoint you."

"I'm not like him. I don't lie or go back on promises. I say what I mean and mean what I say. I will draw the line at murder in cold blood—reluctantly," he pronounced with disdain. "But Midas will pay for all he's done, Ilona. To you and to me. He'll pay until he has absolutely nothing left. I swear that to you."

A bitter wind passed over her heart, making her shiver inside.

He meant it. She felt it. For the first time she believed *in* him. Unequivocally. He wouldn't stop until Midas was on his knees.

That ought to be satisfying, but she was disturbed by his vow. She was, paradoxically, afraid for him. She was afraid of what he would lose along the way. Midas would make sure Leander didn't come away unscathed. More concerning, Midas had a way of causing a person to twist themselves in ugly ways. Look at Hercules, deeply unhappy, never standing up for his own principles and often dispatched to do Midas's dirty work. Perpetually miserable.

Even she had become a crumpled form of herself, too fearful of further dents to let herself be all that she could be.

She didn't know how to articulate that worry in a way he might accept, though. And they had arrived at his building. His warm hand closed over hers as they walked up and that innocuous contact had the ability to empty her brain of all those worries.

In fact, a girlish lightness entered her heart. They were going on a *date*.

It became their habit to go out for dinner every night. It was both a low stress event and high. They went to quiet, intimate places and talked about the wedding and travel and foods they liked. In that way it was companionable and easy.

But Leander did courtly things, holding her chair and asking her to dance.

Every time Ilona was in his arms, she struggled to hide that his spicy scent and the brush of his body made her bones weak, but she never refused. It was the most delicious torture to put herself through. She liked feeling his strength and his confidence as he led her around the floor. She liked how cherished she felt when his thumb brushed the heel of her palm or his splayed fingers shifted on her waist, strong and possessive.

It always made her long for him to kiss her or make a move when they got home, but he always stayed well on his side of the wide bed they continued to share.

Tonight, as he seated her and took her wrap, his thumb brushed into the hollow beneath her ear. His caress sent a tingling rush into her breasts.

"No makeup tonight. That's good."

The bruises, she realized with a sick lurch in her stomach. They had finally faded and she was glad they were gone, but there were plenty of other reminders of that dark night—the police report that had gone nowhere because Midas had an alibi, the fresh rumors Odessa had started about Ilona being in financial straits, the RSVPs to the wedding that were weighted far more heavily to Leander's guests than to hers.

Leander's warm hand gave her shoulder a squeeze. Affection? Reassurance?

It was gone too quickly for her to interpret. He circled the table, leaving her in a confusion of shy pleasure. He'd become difficult to read, offering those small, unexpected caresses before withdrawing. They left her bereft and swimming in yearning. She kept waiting for the fiery desire he'd shown her on the yacht to reemerge, but each time it sparked, he always seemed to douse it and move away.

While she quietly drowned in unrequited lust.

He paused with his hand on his chair and she looked up at him with her heart in her throat, wondering if he had any clue of her feelings. His handsomeness nearly undid her, with his alert profile, his tall bearing and wide shoulders, his nail beds going white as he tightened his grip on the back of his chair—

With a gasp, she swung her head around, expecting Midas to be swooping down at them, but it was only a woman of fiftyish years.

Oh! She had completely forgotten.

Ilona rose and smiled in flustered greeting. Now she felt extra foolish for the way she was mooning over Leander, but she was excited to have arranged this little surprise for him.

Her flashing glance revealed he was staring coldly at the woman, his mouth held in a grim line.

Ilona's stomach plummeted and her blood went ice-cold in her veins. She'd made a mistake. A terrible one.

But Susan Vasilou was upon them, the moment unavoidable. Her hair was dark brunette with shots of silver, her build slight and graceful, her mouth wide like her son's as she smiled in a way that struck Ilona as being forcibly bright.

"Darling." She touched Leander's arm and offered her cheek.

"Mother." He bussed her cheek and shot a glower at Ilona. "You invited her?"

"I—" Culpability had to be painted all over her face.

"Oh, don't scold her. I asked her to let me surprise you." Susan tapped his wrist. "Yes, I'm joining them," she told the server who appeared beside her.

While a chair and place setting were procured, Leander said, "I thought we would see you at the rehearsal dinner tomorrow."

"I wanted a chance to have you all to myself." Susan held out her hand to Ilona. "And to meet your beautiful bride. Please call me Susan." Her Greek lilted with her British accent, but it was smooth and unhesitating.

Leander politely helped both of them with their chairs. This time, he didn't touch Ilona as he did. He radiated so much irritation, her toes curled in her shoes with anxiety.

"Tell me about the wedding." Susan turned her eager interest on Ilona. "How did you two meet? Tell me *everything.*"

Ilona practically choked on her tongue. Where to start? Not with the truth.

"Using Ilona is beneath you, Mother," Leander said in a chilly undertone as they were left alone. "If you want to see me or know something about my life, call *me.*"

"But you so rarely pick up," Susan said mildly. "And I'm genuinely interested in the woman who has captured your heart."

I haven't, Ilona silently moaned. If anything, she had alienated Leander by making an assumption. She had blindsided him when she was supposed to be earning his trust. *I'm sorry*, she tried to telegraph, but he had averted his grim expression to glare at the view of the Parthenon.

"I'm sorry I didn't make the engagement party. Your family must have thought it odd." Susan slid a wounded glance toward Leander that Ilona interpreted to mean she hadn't been invited.

Why was he so hostile toward her? In their brief telephone conversation, Susan had struck Ilona as charming and likable, not cruel or objectionable. Did she overspend or speak out of turn after a few drinks? What?

"My family wasn't there, either," Ilona volunteered, wading carefully through the thick undercurrents. "My mother passed when I was young and my father died last year. My relationship with the rest is extremely difficult. I don't expect you'll meet them at all." Not if she could help it.

"I'm so sorry." Susan sounded sincere. Compassionate. "Every bride should have a family member who is as excited as she is. Allow me." She propped her chin on her hand. "I adore talking about gowns and floral arrangements. Do you have a theme?"

Ilona couldn't help it. She *liked* her. Conversation flowed easily between them and the meal would have been very pleasant if Leander had warmed up a degree or two, but he remained withdrawn, barely speaking.

While they were waiting for dessert, Ilona excused herself to the powder room, thinking to give them a moment to clear the air.

"I'll come with you." Susan rose at the same time.

"Really, Mother?" Leander gave Susan a frosted look.

"Are you afraid we'll talk about you?" she chided.

"I know you will. Whatever you have to say can be said here, to my face." He nodded at her chair.

They held some sort of contest of wills, one that made Ilona feel she had caused this discord between them. She nearly wilted back into her chair in miserable defeat.

"It's all things you've heard before, darling. What difference would it make where I say it?" Susan sounded almost anguished, but she quickly covered that impression with a warm smile for Ilona. She tucked her arm through Ilona's and steered her toward the ladies' lounge.

Ilona's heart was heavy when they returned to the penthouse. She was in the oddest position of wanting to know Leander's side of things while wanting to defend his mother. She wanted to ask questions, but given his shuttered expression, she also wanted to respect his privacy. She settled on a sincere apology.

"I should have mentioned that she would be joining us. She called to welcome me to the family and I invited her on impulse. She said she wanted to surprise you so I…" Put him into a situation he didn't want. "I'm very sorry. It didn't occur to me you wouldn't want to see her."

The whole point in "dating" had been to get to know each other, but as she looked back on their half-dozen dinners, she realized they hadn't revealed anything deeply personal. She knew his taste in music was eclectic and he preferred snow skiing over water skiing, but she didn't know what his childhood had been like.

So much for honest and open communication.

"She manipulated you. Be on guard for it in future," he warned crisply. "Take everything she told you with a bucket of salt. And don't pretend she didn't try to pull you to her side when she got you alone."

She had, but Ilona didn't feel manipulated. She felt sorry for her. Sad for both of them.

"Do you want one?" Leander was pouring himself a drink.

"Thank you." She didn't really want it. Most nights she changed and they spent the rest of the evening working on their laptops or watching television. Tonight, she curled up on the sofa and accepted the glass he handed her, gently asking, "Will you tell me your side of it?"

"What's to tell? She didn't want to be a mother, didn't want a relationship with me when I was a child and needed her, but now she expects my attention and affection. I send her money to ensure she lives comfortably. I don't know why that isn't enough."

Because Susan was lonely and regretful and had been in a no-win situation from the start, if even a smidge of what she had told Ilona was true.

"You were eight when she moved back to London?" she pried carefully.

"To star in a musical. Not even a particularly good one. Her career has always been more down than up, but she insisted on pursuing it." His tone was dismissive.

"That's entertainment, I think. Eternally hoping for the big break." And wasn't everyone entitled to dream? "Perhaps she was homesick. I used to suffer it quite badly."

"When you were at boarding school?" He looked over his shoulder from the window.

"When I came to live with my father."

He made a noncommittal noise and returned to glowering at the city lights.

"It sounds like she was very young when she had you."

"They both were. My father managed to stick around so I don't see why she couldn't."

I got pregnant on holiday, Susan had told her, adding with a papery laugh, *I don't know how. Leander's father was so shy he could barely speak to me, but we had a little fling. I felt so grown-up until I was forced to grow up. My mother told me I'd better hope he married me because she wouldn't have an unwed mother in her house.*

"I have to ask…" Ilona bit her lip. Her own mother hadn't left her by choice so it wasn't particularly fair to say this, but, "Would you be as judgmental if your father had gone away to pursue his career?"

"He involved me in it," he said flatly, adding with scathing sarcasm, "But I take your point. My desire to star in musicals is nonexistent. It's my fault I didn't see her most of my life."

Ah. Well, then. She looked into her drink. "She never asked you to join her?"

"What was the point? I would have been at school during the day. She worked nights and weekends. We wouldn't have seen one another."

He and Niko were so close, Susan had lamented. *Leander wanted to stay here with his father so I didn't fight for him. I don't think he's ever forgiven me for that.*

Leander swore and squeezed the back of his neck. "I know it's childish to resent her. You're right. A father can absent himself without such harsh judgment, but she made a lot of promises to me that never panned out. She took the support my father sent her, but never took *me.*

When I told her that Midas was offering to take our software to market, she encouraged us to trust him. She wanted the financial benefit of what Midas promised without having done any of the work to earn it."

Not unlike Midas, Ilona inferred. And the promised benefits hadn't arrived. Leander must have felt so foolish when he realized that Midas had tricked them. It was natural to look for someone to blame. He probably thought that if his mother had cautioned him, instead of encouraging him, he might not have lost everything.

"When I found— When my father died, she didn't turn up until the funeral service."

Found. Oh, no. She hadn't known that part. "I'm so sorry, Leander."

He shook off her murmur of sympathy.

"But—" Ilona frowned. "I was under the impression she arrived right away."

"Is that what she told you?"

"Not explicitly. It was just an impression," she mused, recollecting Susan's anguish.

He didn't cry, not even at the service, he was so traumatized. He didn't say a word to me until it was all over.

"*Then* she wanted me to come live with her," he said bitterly. "But she didn't have anything to offer me, just a flat-share and a poorly executed dream. My father had had to stop sending her support after Midas's trickery so we were both completely broke. The house had been mortgaged to finance the development of our technology. It was already in foreclosure. My father had legal bills from trying to sue Midas for what was ours. The stress and failure were so heavy on him..." He slugged back most of his drink.

He'll never forgive me for not being here, but I didn't love Niko. Not the way a wife should. Marrying so young, I felt cheated of the life I should have had. I kept thinking I would prove my dreams were worth the time I had invested in them, but I never have. Not in Leander's eyes. Somehow, I turned into my mother. I caused my own child to resent me. By the time Niko was gone, Leander wanted nothing to do with me.

"Did your father love her?" Ilona asked curiously.

"Yes." No hesitation. It was a fact delivered with a side of scorn.

Her heart felt stretched completely out of shape then, for all of them.

"He never looked at another woman and always said he wanted her to be happy. He let her disappear and keep his name and his money... But he was miserable without her. He didn't say it, but I could see it. How could she expect that I would side with her when she had treated him that way?"

"She let him raise her son, though. It's fine that you're angry with her, Leander, but surely it counts for something that she didn't make you live away from him? She said you wanted to be here with your father so she didn't fight for you. That you never wanted to come see her so she quit asking."

She could only see his profile, but his expression twisted with distaste.

"Is it such a crime that she wanted to live where *she* chose? On her own terms?" Ilona could relate to that; she really could.

His body seemed to bunch up with tension.

She braced herself to have her head bitten off, but he shrugged away whatever impact her remark had made.

"Maybe I would have had more sympathy

for her if she hadn't lived off my father all that time. Off of me." He turned and jabbed his chest. "I sent her home with what I got from selling the little I had left. Then I hired on with a remote labor camp and sent her half my paycheck. I still support her. So tell me again how that makes her someone I should respect?"

"Don't then," she said, setting aside her drink and rising to her feet. "Your relationship with your mother is your business. But from my perspective, she didn't mean to hurt you. She was young and idealistic and misguided. Maybe she didn't show her love the way you wanted her to, but she does love you. I would have given anything to have had that much, rather than the mother figure I had in Odessa who destroyed my self-esteem. Enjoy nursing your grudge. I'm going to bed."

CHAPTER TEN

ILONA WASN'T ENTIRELY WRONG, which was irksome.

Leander much preferred to sit atop his high horse, but at thirty-two, he had to feel some pity for his parents, both a very young twenty when he had been born. They couldn't have been prepared for the responsibility. His father, nerdy and chronically anxious, had still been at university. His mother had struggled to make friends in her new country because her husband had been reluctant to leave the house. When she had suggested they all move to England, his father had outright refused. He hadn't liked change of any kind.

Ilona's remark about suffering homesickness as a child had briefly diverted him from wondering if his mother had experienced it, too. He hated to think of how powerless and lost Ilona must have felt at five, when she'd gone to live with a stranger who failed to fully care for her.

At least he'd had his mother for eight years. She had stayed until Leander's father earned his doctorate, then she had given her own aspirations eight years. Perhaps she would have come back on her own if his father hadn't passed, but they would never know. Leander hadn't given her a chance to make overtures in the subsequent sixteen years.

That remark Ilona had made about his mother coming to Greece before the funeral was niggling at him. Had she arrived sooner? He genuinely couldn't remember those blurry days. They all bled into one another.

Very quickly, as a means of dealing with his grief and guilt, he had focused on revenge. The first step had been to make money. Fast. He had lied about his age and gotten on with a company that wanted a strong back willing to fly to remote locations and push a wheelbarrow full of wet cement. The mindless work had allowed him to plot meticulously how he would rise to Midas's level, then take him down.

Thanks to working next to his father's broad education in science, Leander had known a little about everything. He had quickly become an on-site resource for any sort of technical question. If he hadn't known the answer, he knew how to find it. Soon he'd worked his way up to being flown out to solve oddball problems on difficult projects.

The bean counters had always wanted the fastest, cheapest solution, however. They had never looked at the greater costs. The need for a company that would use greener technologies became glaringly obvious, but cultural mind-sets were hard to change from within. He had started his own company and, by then, had known enough people in the industry he had been able to cherry-pick the ones who didn't need convincing. They had embraced his mind-set and he'd been on a growth trajectory ever since.

Through those years, he hadn't let anyone— including his mother—distract him from his goal. Maybe he had held on to his resentment toward her so he wouldn't feel guilty about holding her at a distance. That's also why he'd sent her money, to soothe his conscience.

When he had finally started his own business ten years ago, she had tried to give him all his money back, revealing that she had saved every penny he'd sent her.

He'd been *furious*. She hadn't made herself more comfortable all this time and she hadn't invested it properly either, leaving it to gather anemic interest in a daily savings account. Most excruciating, however, was that it had been hard for him to send that money to her. It had been hard to earn and hard to part with it when his desire to wreak his vengeance against Midas consumed him.

But she hadn't seemed to value what he'd sent or even to want it. That had *hurt*.

He used a swallow of alcohol to burn away the ache in his chest.

It was childish to still feel a sting over that. He'd made her buy a flat with it and now, at least, she didn't have to suffer eccentric roommates and other inconveniences.

He almost heard Ilona ask, "Why would you care if she suffers?"

Because he was his father's son. He understood that he had a responsibility toward his mother and lived up to it, regardless of his feelings toward her. That's all this was. He did his duty and he didn't need her buying him cardigans or asking whether he'd seen a dentist in some pretense that she cared. He wanted her to stay out of his way and out of his life.

She'd caused Ilona to light up, though, making all the right noises over mention of Venetian lace and calla lilies. Leander had left all the wedding decisions to his bride and, as he had listened, had realized there were a disgusting number of them. It had meant a lot to Ilona that his mother had applauded all the choices she had made. He'd seen shy pleasure glowing within her under the simple praise.

Meanwhile, *her* stepmother had been the subject of a security meeting. How would Odessa be escorted from the house if she tried to crash the ceremony? Would the police be called for her? Or only if Midas turned up?

Leander's mother might be clumsy with her affection and was maybe a little too self-involved, but Ilona had made a fair point. His mother didn't intentionally hurt anyone. If she wanted someone to fuss over, and Ilona wanted to receive that fuss, Leander shouldn't stand in the way of it. He would have to make clear that Ilona wasn't to be toyed with, of course. If his mother extended a friendship, she couldn't disappear in eight days or eight years, leaving Ilona as abandoned as he'd felt.

He glanced at the clock, deciding he had waited long enough. Ilona ought to be asleep.

Sleeping beside her was pure torture. Sharing his home with her was, but in the best possible way. Her aromatic products lingered in the bathroom after her shower, imprinting on his brain for the day. Her phone and laptop looked very feminine and cute next to his meatier electronics when she left them in the office to charge. She *snored*, but softly, like a kitten purring. Her weight barely made a dent on the far side of the bed, she never stole the covers, but he struggled to fall asleep or stay asleep because he couldn't stop thinking about the way she'd shattered against his touch on the yacht.

It was rare to have that sort of connection. He was dying to explore it more deeply. Pun intended.

Stop, he ordered himself, and ran his hand down his face.

Every night, as he lay awake beside her, he resolved to buy a bed for one of the other rooms. Then he woke beside her and *liked* it.

It didn't make sense. He wasn't a cuddler.

He had always found having another body in the bed too hot. He didn't like the sense that someone was so close to him while he was unguarded, but with Ilona, he was the one on guard. He had developed a subconscious alertness to any danger that might approach her and he only relaxed when she was in his sight or sleeping beside him. When he knew she was safe.

She seemed to sleep soundly there, too, which also pleased him. She'd been jumpy and anxious that first night, as anyone would be, and continued to have tense moments. When he stepped close, she often went very still, seeming to hold her breath as though uncertain what he would do to her. That always disturbed him enough to have him moving away. He didn't want to intimidate her. He wanted her to be comfortable with him, to know he would never hurt her.

If Midas hadn't terrified her out of her mind, he might have reopened the sex question, but that would have to wait until… Hell. Hopefully not three years from now.

He drained his glass and set it aside, then quietly entered the bedroom.

* * *

Ilona was still mulling over everything she had learned about Leander when he entered the bedroom. He paused as he saw her sitting in the pool of lamplight, chin on the mountain of her updrawn knees.

She lifted her head, pulse tripping. She was usually fast asleep by the time he came to bed.

"I didn't think you'd still be up," he said, closing the door and tugging at his tie. "Is something wrong?"

"Just thinking."

"About my mother? I'm over it."

She'd been contemplating more than that, but as he threw his tie toward a chair her brain blanked entirely. Was he going to strip in front of her like one of those exotic dancers? *Okay.*

"I'll call her tomorrow and lay out some ground rules. I don't want her asking you about my private life, but if you two want to go for brunch or text each other cat videos, do so with my blessing."

"Where does picking out wallpaper fall? Too personal? Or...?" She waved her hands in the air, blinking with innocence.

He only gave her a flat stare, not seeming to enjoy the joke.

She bit her lips in compunction. "Thank you. I like her. And I feel for her, chasing something that never panned out the way she wanted it to. That's hard for anyone. She's really proud of you, you know. That you were able to make your own dream come true."

He paused in dragging his shirt free of his trousers. "My company isn't a *dream*. It's a means to an end."

Midas. He really was a four-letter word.

"Don't you think he takes up too much real estate in our heads?" She'd been thinking that a lot lately. "I think the best revenge would be to forget about him altogether and live our lives without his shadow hanging over us."

"Give up now? When I'm so close to squashing him like a bug?" Leander pulled his belt free and threw it after his tie. "Is that what you want to do? Let him get away with everything he's done?"

He sounded so aggressive, she pressed back into the pillows.

"No. But chasing revenge allows him to win in other ways. We can't be happy if we're angry and we deserve to be happy." She saw that so clearly now, how she had refused to allow herself real happiness because there had always been this dark fret that Midas would punish her for so much as a smile. He probably would continue to try to spoil her fun, but that didn't mean she should do his harmful work for him. "He shouldn't be allowed to steal our moments of pleasure from us."

Leander hung his hands on his hips and stared at her a moment, then he toed off his shoes, muttering, "I'm a little too drunk for this conversation."

"Am I making you angry? I'm not defending him." He didn't even *seem* drunk.

"No," he said dryly. "But my mind leapt to our little moment of pleasure on the yacht. The fact he stole your ability to enjoy that sort of thing only fans my flames of hatred."

"Oh." A blast of fiery heat burst alive within her, part alarm, part acute self-consciousness, part remembered ecstasy. "You, um…" She swallowed. "You think about that?"

He stopped halfway to the bathroom, shirt loose and open, feet bare. "Did you think I could forget it?"

"I don't know." She rubbed her chin on her knee. "We had that argument after and you've been so reserved ever since, not even hinting that you were interested in me that way."

"Because you were assaulted." He shoved his hands into his pockets. "You need to know I can control myself."

She did know that. Or rather, she had never thought he couldn't. She had moments when she felt vulnerable around him, but emotionally, not the kind of vulnerable where she didn't want to be trapped in an elevator with him.

His voice plummeted to a dark rasp that sounded as though it originated in his chest. "Do *you* think about it?"

"I don't know what you're talking about," she blurted, then dropped her guilty face onto her knees, hiding her culpable blush.

He gave a snort of amusement.

"I do think about it," she conceded, blushing harder as she lifted her head. Her voice thinned with plaintive emotion as she forced herself into that open honest place they were trying so reluctantly to find. "I think about it and about what I just said, that I don't want to live my life in reaction to what Midas might do.

I don't want to think about him *at all*. I want to think about what *I* want." She hugged her knees even tighter into her chest.

Leander's cheeks went hollow. He stood rooted and still, as though carved from oak. "And what do you want?" he inquired.

Here she was leaping off a cliff again, this time of her own volition. Air rushed around her and her breath was gone. Her body braced for the icy plunge into the unknown.

But this yearning in her was too soul-deep to keep it contained. "I want a baby."

He swayed like a tree sustaining a hard gust. "You said—"

"I know what I said and that stands," she rushed to say. "I don't want a baby out of spite. I want a child. A family. And before you offer to make one with me, I need you to think about what that would really mean, Leander. Not what it would do to Midas, but what it would do to *you*. Especially…" She bit the corner of her mouth again. "Especially coming from parents who separated because they couldn't make it work."

He sucked air through his teeth and looked away. "That is completely different."

"No, it's not. We're *planning* to split up. Plenty of couples divorce with little impact on their children, but we would have to figure out how to do that before we start down that road."

He was still an inscrutable monolith, profile craggy and shadowed, jaw clamped tight.

"Or not," she mumbled, shrinking into her hunched shoulders. "I don't want you to have a baby with me for any reason than that you want one. Please don't agree otherwise, but…" Now she was floundering in the foam, getting knocked about by the choppy waves, unable to fully orient herself, but casting out for that final other thing she wanted. "I thought you should know that I'm open to it. And that…" She searched his profile, wishing she could see inside his head. "That even if you don't want children, I want…" She couldn't seem to swallow. Her throat had constricted too much. "I would like a real marriage. If you do," she ended in another rush.

"Sex." He grunted out the word like a caveman, swiveling his head to pin her to the bed. "You want sex. Unprotected sex."

Her heart was thudding so loud, she thought

he must hear it across the room, calling to him like a drumbeat.

"Only if you do." She wanted to die. To smother herself in the pillows around her, but she was unable to move, unable to tear her eyes from his edgy, wolfish expression.

"I do." He sauntered toward her, holding her gaze. When he was close enough, he cupped her cheek.

She didn't pull back. In fact, his touch felt so good, her eyes fluttered closed for a moment. When she opened them, her whole body was trembling with nerves. A bigger jolt went through her as she read the hunger in his eyes, completely undisguised.

She might have been alarmed by that glimpse of unfettered lust, but he wasn't making any other move beyond caressing her cheek with his thumb, letting her see the intensity of his desire and that he could control it.

"I, um—" She could hardly form words. Her lips were nerveless, her voice a wavering sound in her throat. "I thought we could wait until our wedding night, though?"

"Quaint." His mouth twisted ruefully and he dropped his hand to his side.

"Only because…" She had to tell him. Had to. But she was worried about his reaction. Would he laugh? Dismiss her? There was only one way to find out. "I'm kind of a virgin."

Leander's soul briefly left his body before he slammed back to his earthly form in a discordant rush.

"Kind of?" he repeated.

"I am," Ilona confirmed, chin tucking defensively. "The yacht was the farthest I've ever gone with anyone."

"You've never had sex. With anyone." Leander couldn't match up the sensually abandoned woman who had exploded in his arms, the woman who had recalibrated his gauge for pleasure, the one who haunted his dreams every night, with the words that had just come out of her mouth.

"Correct."

"Then why the hell did you have that screen for STIs?" He wasn't modest, but the questions and exam were pretty damned personal. She shouldn't have put herself through all that when he hadn't even asked for it.

"I was mad at you," she said to her manicure.

"And it wasn't your business until I decided it was your business."

Such an exasperating woman. He frowned, compelled to ask, "How old are you?"

"Twenty-four. And it's not that I'm against sex before marriage. It's Midas. I've spent my whole life denying myself, worried that every little thing I want to do will only bring negative attention from my family. It's *my* body. If I want to have sex, I can have sex." Her back shot straight and her chin thrust out with defiance.

"Agreed," he said, more at a loss than he'd ever been in his life.

"And if I'm going to have sex, it should be with someone who…" She cleared her throat. "Makes me want to have sex. Right?" The dignity and logic she was using to hide her discomfiture was adorable.

"You're talking about me, right?" He pointed at himself. "I'm the one who makes you want to knock boots?"

"If you're laughing at me, then definitely not you."

"I'm not." He was laughing at the situation and only because he was so astonished. Very little got by him, yet she continued to shake up his presumptions about her.

"Can I ask you one more thing?" Her dark eyes went wide with vulnerability.

"Anything," he assured her, unable to think of one thing she could ask him that would ruin his elation.

"I won't be mad," she insisted, "but I have to know so please be honest. Do you want *me*? Or is this just about Midas?"

An arctic wind seemed to gust through him, chasing out the tenderness that had crept into his heart. All the cracks and fractures inside him began to ache.

"Everything is about Midas," he said with brutal honesty.

She flinched, but nodded acceptance of that.

He didn't like hurting her, but, "I wouldn't be marrying you if you weren't who you are. You're tempting as hell, Ilona. I would have *wanted* to date you if we had met some other way, but I can't waver from the course I've set. If you weren't part of my attack on him, you would have been a distraction. An obstacle. I would have pushed my attraction aside and stayed focused on him."

She was biting the inside of her lip, lashes hiding her eyes, nodding convulsively.

"You wouldn't trust me if I lied and said something different," he ground out.

"I don't think I would have believed you if you had said anything different." Her tone had gone hollow. Her face had lost its rosy color.

Her words were a hard kick, one that cooled his blood.

"After, though. After I've dealt with him, this marriage will only be about us."

"You just told me why it will *never* be about us. Midas will be baked into our vows." Her eyes were glistening as she looked up at him. "And you don't know how long it will take to be satisfied that he's paid enough," she noted sadly. "It could take years. Decades."

"True." He didn't hesitate to deliver that harsh reality, either. "But you told me once that you pick your battles. This one I'm in with him is worth having."

She shrugged, not seeming convinced.

He would prove it to her, though. And they would both live happier lives once he did.

CHAPTER ELEVEN

THE MORNING OF the rehearsal dinner, they convened with their lawyers in Leander's office tower where they signed the appropriate contracts including the one for their new home.

Ursula had found them something in Glyfada, a seven-bedroom contemporary villa with all the amenities, an established staff and gardens that created a shroud of privacy without walling them in. It was almost boxy in design and seemed made strictly from glass and polished marble, but it was bright and welcoming and the view of the infinity pool blended into the horizon so the property appeared to extend into the sea. The decorating would be finished while they were on their honeymoon and they would move in on their return.

Ilona was of two minds about that. She was excited for it, because it was such a lovely property, but she liked sharing her husband's bed. Would they make love then part ways every night? The question was plaguing her, but she hadn't found the courage to ask.

As they stood and shook hands all around, Leander asked Androu and Feodor to wait while he pulled Ilona into a small studio apartment adjacent to his office. Ilona was so distracted by the utilitarian space, she didn't immediately take in what he said.

"I want to make this official right now."

Ilona dragged her eyes off the wide bed. "Make what official?"

"Our marriage. All the paperwork is done, the license is good. There's an officiant waiting to join us."

"You want to get married *right now*?"

"You object?" His gaze narrowed keenly.

Her stomach somersaulted. He still didn't trust her, even after all she'd told him about herself and invited him to make a baby with her.

"I wasn't expecting this." Obviously. She had a feeling that was his purpose in springing it on her, to test her. That hurt, but even more than that, "I'm not...wearing my gown," she mumbled in a small voice, feeling silly for being so excited about wearing it. She rarely let herself truly shine, though. She had pulled out all the stops for tomorrow.

"You look lovely," he stated, dismissing that detail.

She looked down at her bone-colored skirt suit and pale pink blouse, mostly so he wouldn't read the depth of her hurt and disappointment. She looked as though she was attending a business meeting, which she was. That's all their marriage was. A merger. She really was a silly fool for thinking it could be anything else.

"Tomorrow will go ahead as planned," Leander assured her. "But in case it doesn't…"

Midas. Always Midas.

Ilona forced a smile past the ache that had arrived in her throat. "Of course. Let's close this deal."

If he found her remark as cold as his own behavior, she didn't see it. She led him back into his office.

Androu invited the officiant in and the ceremony commenced without ceremony, with only their two assistants in attendance.

For a moment, Ilona consoled herself that it was better this way. She had been worried all the pageantry of speaking her vows in front of a crowd would play on her nerves, but it was actually worse in this little office where the silence of their surprised witnesses was intensely meaningful. They watched her grow emotional as the weight of her words caused her voice to shake and her eyes to fill.

The words weren't even particularly sentimental, just legal statements about the contract of marriage imbuing obligations and responsibilities that she must promise to uphold. Still, when Leander cupped her face and repeated them in his deep rumble, she had to bite her lips to keep them from quivering.

This was big. Profound. If she had had any lingering worries or fears about going through with this marriage, they no longer mattered because it was done. She was tied to this man who claimed he would never hurt her. She believed that, to a point. She was confident he wouldn't attack her physically or deride her, but as she looked into his eyes and the skin on her heart grew paper thin, she knew he could destroy her emotionally.

Because she was more than susceptible to him. She was growing to care for him. Deeply. She wanted him to care for her in the same way, but she didn't believe he was capable of it. Even if he was, he would refuse to let himself care too deeply because of who she was. Because he was too obsessed with Midas.

If you weren't part of my attack on him, you would have been a distraction.

It was heartbreaking to realize all of that, but then he lowered his head and kissed her. His lips brushed across hers, tender and sweet enough to cause a colorful explosion behind her closed eyelids. For a few precious seconds, she was convinced they were soul mates.

Then he drew back and the moment was gone. There were more handshakes. Feodor gave her a misty hug and said something about how it was a relief to know that if anything went wrong tomorrow, at least the most important part had already happened.

It hadn't, though, Ilona realized with a lurch of her heart. She caught Leander—her *husband*—looking at her with banked hunger and it struck her like a wrecking ball that her wedding night had arrived a day early.

Leander watched Ilona kick off her shoes as they stepped off the elevator into the penthouse.

He tried to catch her eye to read her mood, but she wasn't allowing it.

"I suppose I can use this time between now and dinner to pack for the honeymoon," she said in a tone that was not nearly as casual as she was likely striving for. She had mentioned going into her office this afternoon, but Feodor had looked at her like she was out of her tree and assured her there was nothing so pressing it couldn't wait.

Leander had sworn the pair to secrecy and brought her home, high on the triumph of being able to call her his wife. Strangely, his satisfaction went beyond vengeance. He was thrilled in deeply primitive, remarkably possessive ways. She was *his*.

He could tell she was still taken aback by his change in plan, though.

"You're angry with me," Leander surmised.

"No. Why would I be?"

"Because I didn't tell you what I wanted to do."

"Because you didn't trust me to go through with the wedding tomorrow," she extrapolated. "You don't trust me."

"I can't," he said bluntly, steeling himself

against the bloom of hurt in her eyes. "The dominoes I've set in place are so delicate, it would only take one false breath to wreck it all."

"Don't tell me what else you're planning, then. Let it be a surprise for me as well as him." She moved into the bedroom, peeling off her jacket as she went.

Leander sighed, but he had no regret. The cascade toward Midas's downfall would start now and there was nothing the other man could do about it.

Midas would try, of course. Leander had no doubt about that. There would be some attempt to disrupt tomorrow's wedding, but it would not only fail, Midas would expose himself as the villain he was.

That was the first prong of Leander's attack. The second was to put the screws on Midas financially. Midas lived beyond his means— which was saying something considering the depth of the family fortune. Most of his assets were either leveraged to the hilt or bought on credit he couldn't pay down. Leander had been quietly positioning himself to buy up the other man's debts and loans so he could call them. That, too, began tomorrow.

The third and fourth tine on his barbed fork were aimed at Hercules and Odessa. By taking them out, Midas would lose his most loyal supporters and have little to fall back on.

Hercules had made himself an easy target by spending the last two years painting for a gallery showing. The gallery in question had recently been purchased by a shell company owned by Leander. It would close its doors indefinitely, locking all of Hercules's work inside, tying up any funds or acclaim he might have earned from those sales. Hercules could sue to have them released, but it would cost him a pretty penny to do so.

As for Odessa, did she think she was the only one who could grind gossip through the rumor mill? Misuse of charity funds wasn't even an unfounded lie. Leander literally had the receipts showing a profound difference in the actual costs of catering and the amount claimed against the raised donations. All of Odessa's pet caterers and planners would think twice about allowing her stink to attach itself to their reputations in future.

Within a few weeks, the entire family would be in such a shambles it would be an easy sell to the board that Leander should take Midas's place at the helm of Pagonis—especially if his wife was carrying the heir to the company by then.

I don't want you to have a baby with me for any reason than that you want one.

He did want one. Ilona might not believe it, but he wasn't thinking of their child as an instrument of vengeance. Only as a signpost of where the future was headed. Ilona's children would inherit the company and thus the board's allegiance should fall to her.

More than that, he wanted a baby for *her*. She wasn't the spoiled heiress he had originally judged her. She was privileged, but deprived. Strong as hell, yet vulnerable. Isolated. He wanted to give her the family she craved.

He wanted to give her things no one else had. Freedom from fear. Security. *Orgasms.*

He closed his eyes, still astounded she hadn't had any lovers. It was a crime that she had denied herself all this time and, if he delved around in his bucket of motivation, he knew his rush to marry her wasn't purely about revenge, either. He *wanted* her.

Why? He didn't harbor any secret fetishes for an untouched innocent.

But something about being with her while she discovered her sexuality pleased him. It turned him on and made him feel protective and indulgent and proud. It made him *hungry*. He wanted to show her everything they could do, make her tremble and moan and cry out in joy.

Maybe he did have a secret fetish.

Maybe he just wanted to have sex with a woman who had been on his mind constantly from the moment he'd met her.

He followed her to the bedroom.

Ilona was in a state of confused anticipation. She *was* angry with Leander. She was hurt that he didn't trust her. She was also nervous.

They were married. That meant they could have sex. Which wasn't to say she had been waiting for some sort of permission. She had only set that deadline because she was so darned *daunted* by the prospect and now that excuse was gone.

Which didn't put her off. She wanted to sleep

with him. They had hours before the rehearsal
dinner. A prickly heat coated her skin with
something akin to urgency, but what if she
wasn't good at it? What if they were both disappointed? The first time was always said to
be a letdown. Anticlimactic.

Who had come up with *that* stupid pun?

How did she even make overtures to get
things started? What would he think of her if
she did?

She was standing in her robe, trying to work
out what to put on so she might look enticing
without looking desperate, when the bedroom
door opened and he came to prop his shoulder
against the open door of the closet.

"There's this thing I've heard married couples do," he drawled.

She sucked in a breath so loud his mouth
twitched.

"It's called kissing and making up."

Make-up sex? Was that what she wanted her
first time to be?

She hugged herself and stared into a hollow
space between where her clothes hung beside
his.

He sobered. "We don't have to do anything

you don't want to do, Ilona. But we need to talk this out."

"I'm not angry," she insisted. "Not really. I'm…" Pressure built in her chest, then the words came out in a rush. "I'm scared. I'm afraid that if you don't trust me, it means I can't trust you. And now look what I've done." She was married to him. She was going to start sleeping with him. She was going to be more physically defenseless than it was possible to be.

She was also afraid of what he could do to her, what he was starting to make her feel. She feared becoming dependent on him for confidence and pleasure and self-worth. For a reason to wake in the morning.

"Believe it or not, I'm trying to protect you," he said gravely. "All of the actions I'm taking from now on are mine. He can't accuse you or blame you if you have no part in it, not even knowledge of what I plan to do."

She jerked a shoulder to dismiss that, but she was slightly mollified.

"Let's agree to do one thing for the next few hours," he began.

Her eyes widened and he barked out a laugh.

"Not every word out of my mouth is about sex, Ilona. Relax." He ran his hand over his face, rearranging his amusement into something more kind. "Let's quit talking about him. Or thinking about him. When we're in this room, in our bed, it's only about us."

"That's frightening, too," she realized as she felt the full weight of his attention. It was as though his words had removed an invisible wall that she had been using to hold him off. Now she felt exposed. Defenseless.

"Why?"

Because there was no "us." They didn't have enough between them that wasn't tainted by their history.

Maybe that's what sex was for, though. To build the connection they needed.

With an awkward memory? She rubbed her brow, not relishing making a fool of herself.

"Does it bother you that I don't really know how it all works? I mean, I *know*." She rolled her eyes upward. "I know what happens. I lack *practical* knowledge." Her cheeks were so hot they hurt.

"You seem to be a quick study. I'm not worried."

"Don't laugh at me." She covered her face.

"I'm not. I swear I'm not." He was definitely chuckling as his warm hands came around her wrists and drew them down. "I won't rush you. You can stop me anytime. You know that, don't you?" His quicksilver gaze delved into her own, so deep her insides quavered.

She was barefoot, much shorter than when she wore shoes. She was inundated by emotions, too. Unsure but excited, inadequate but wanting to learn. Safe, but aware this would change things in her. She would feel different about him and herself after this. The intimacy of the act, the way she would have to strip away all her defenses and reveal herself, was terrifying.

But she gave the barest hint of a nod, too overwhelmed to speak.

A smile ghosted across his lips, then he drew her arms up to encourage them to twine around his neck while he pressed his mouth to hers, brushing softly.

It was a chaste kiss. A greeting and a quest. A promise to go slow and wait for her.

It was lovely and for a moment she simply enjoyed it, allowing her fingertips to play against the stubble that faded into a line on the back of his neck.

But her shy desire had been simmering for weeks, ever since that first wild kiss at the restaurant. Their interlude on the yacht had teased her with what could be and now her yearnings were gathering into a tangle with her anxious determination, forming a knot of frustration. He was being too careful. Too slow. She wanted the storm. The hurricane she knew he could deliver. She wanted to be swept away.

She instinctually opened her mouth and pressed more firmly into his kiss, allowing her breasts to squash against the wall of his chest, willing him to plunder.

A small jolt went through him and then his arm firmed around her. He abruptly angled his head to seal their mouths more thoroughly. His other hand cupped the back of her head. He held her where he wanted her as he took. Ravished.

But he gave, too. Oh, he knew how to inject delicious joy into her with the thrust of his tongue and the way he palmed her backside. An electric current formed between all those points of contact, making her nerve endings hum. When he scraped his teeth at her lip, she tightened her arms and rose on tiptoes. He tilted her hips into the thick presence between them, letting her feel his arousal against her mound and she nearly fainted with excitement.

An involuntary moan left her and a grunt of satisfaction left him. He abruptly broke away, leaving her dazed, but he gathered her up and brought her to the bed, setting her there with a dark look of intention in his eyes.

What had she done?

The door was open, the sun pouring through the slats of the blinds, illuminating the bed and her. And him, as he undressed, unhurried and watchful.

She eyed the fine pattern of hair across his chest as it appeared, noted how tight his dark brown nipples were, admired the sheen on his powerful shoulders and the way his taut abdomen held such a well-defined six-pack. She wanted to touch him there. Kiss his navel. Why? What a strange compulsion, but it was real and nearly impossible to resist.

"Take off your robe," he commanded as he dropped his shirt to the floor.

She barely heard him through the rushing in

her ears, but she timidly rose onto her knees and slowly unbelted, watching him watching her. It's like a bathing suit, she tried to tell herself, but it wasn't.

"Tease," he chided with smoky pleasure as shyness slowed her movements and she unwound her hair before she loosened her robe and only let it fall to the point it cut across her shoulders.

He shed his pants and socks without hesitation then made an adjustment to himself inside his briefs. The thick shape of him was obvious, though. Butterflies battered in her middle as she stared at that hidden, mysterious part of him.

Leander joined her, knees splaying wide outside her own demurely closed ones. He finished brushing the silk off her arms so it pooled onto the mattress behind her.

A considering noise rumbled in his chest as he took in her pale yellow bra and matching underwear. His finger dropped one bra strap off her shoulder, then his mouth set itself there, branding the spot with heat and dampness and an electrifying sensation that shot straight into her nipples.

His mouth nuzzled and climbed up her nape, lifting goose bumps on her arms and scalp. Then he was kissing her again, gathering her in his arms as they both rose to kneel in the middle of the bed.

She could hardly breathe, could hardly hold her balance and clung to his shoulders, startlingly weak. It was the onslaught of sensations. Not just the kiss, but the hardness of his flexed muscles beneath her hands and the brush of his skin against hers. The intriguing shape of him and the way his flat hand thrust into the back of her panties and cupped her cheek.

Her stomach turned to jelly and she broke from their kiss to gasp, "This feels really good."

"It does." His deep, rasping voice was as much a part of this seduction as everything else.

She helplessly turned her face into the crook of his neck and her lips parted on instinct, tongue dabbing out to taste his skin.

The hand on her bottom clenched more possessively and a sound rattled in his chest that sent a heady sensation of power through her.

"You like that?"

"You can tell I do."

His briefs were struggling to contain him. She drew back enough to run her hands over his chest and the ripples of his ribs and down to the flat stomach that had called to her a moment ago. He was firm and warm and her thumb followed the trail of flat hairs to his navel.

When her fingertips splayed to the waistband of his briefs, she glanced up at him.

He lifted a brow in laconic invitation to continue.

She swallowed and let her touch stray into his waistband, discovering more heat, velvet and steel, aggressive strength and a power to make him hiss as she explored.

She couldn't believe she was doing this, touching any man like this, let alone Leander. He hated her, didn't he?

Not in this moment. His gray eyes glittered like sunlight on a lake. His mouth was relaxed and each of his exhales was a near purr of enjoyment.

"Like this," he rumbled, pushing his briefs down his thighs.

She was confronted by the sight of his erection, dark with arousal, intimidating yet compelling. She had another impulsive fantasy of taking him into her mouth, wondering what that would feel like, taste like. Wondering if he would like it.

He showed her how he liked to be stroked, guiding her, watching her, then he cupped the side of her neck and kissed her. At the same time, his hand plunged into the front of her underwear and he claimed the slick flesh he found, sending a sharp spike of pleasure through her, wiping her brain.

"Am I doing it right, *glykiá mou*?" he mocked against her gasping mouth. "Show me."

She couldn't speak. She lost her grip on him and her own control as he stroked his two fingers through her folds, returning again and again to tease the knot of nerves in the small vise of his touch.

"Did you think you weren't having this effect on me?" he asked as she pressed her forehead into his collarbone. "How close are you?"

Close. She held herself still for his touch, breath stalled as she chased the pinnacle that his teasing touch kept just out of reach.

She sobbed when he withdrew. She half expected a smug smile at denying her, but he only promised, "Soon."

There was nothing in his face except lust. Unadulterated lust as he finished removing his underwear and dispatched hers as adeptly. He pressed her onto her back.

This was it. She apprehensively parted her legs as he loomed atop her, but after one brief kiss, he began working his way down.

Oh, no. That would be too intimate.

"We can just…do it," she said, playing her fingers through his hair as his mouth went across the top of her chest. He was ready; she was ready. "Don't you want to?"

"I want to do many things, *ateleíoti gynaíka mou*." My endless woman. "Many."

He cupped her breast and licked at her nipple. Blew across the dampness so it tightened hard enough to ache, then enclosed it in the heat of his mouth. Bizarrely, the pull of his mouth sent electric heat into her loins, flooding her with a fresh response of damp arousal.

She found herself writhing beneath him as he anointed both her breasts this way. She slid her thighs against his hard ones, liking the scrape of his leg hair against the softness of her own limbs, arching so he would take her nipple deeper into his mouth.

At one point, he hissed something in a voice that wasn't quite steady and his teeth scraped the side of her breast. Then he was taking his kisses down and down, before parting her and then tasting her and leaving her with no secrets left undiscovered.

He didn't need her to show him anything. Before she could dream of being self-conscious, she was sobbing in the acute pleasure of climax.

That did make her feel abashed, tipping so quickly and easily into her own enjoyment. She felt selfish, but he didn't stop. He stayed exactly where he was, tenderly teasing her back into restless arousal, then growing more determined to make her moan.

When she began lifting her hips into his caress, he slowly made his way back up her body, reacquainting one kiss at a time with all the places he'd already visited.

"What are you doing to me?" she asked, baffled by how much care he seemed to be taking. By how much pleasure he was bestowing upon her with such generosity.

"Enjoying you. Enjoying what we do to each

other. I love the way you're giving yourself over to me, letting me claim all of you as mine."

Her overheated brain tripped on his *I love*, but she didn't have time to become despondent that it wasn't a more profound declaration. He swept his hand down between them, before plunging a finger into the molten core of her, making her shake.

They kissed passionately and when she lifted her hips into his touch, he shifted to settle over her.

"I'm not wearing a condom," he reminded against her lips, guiding the blunt tip of his erection against her entrance.

"I know," she whispered, legs helplessly falling open even farther.

He watched her as he pressed into her. It was too much. She wanted to close her eyes against that intense look of his, but she couldn't make herself do it. She gripped his upper arms and bit her bottom lip and tried not to wince at the sting that grew to a white-hot warning of true pain. A small sound of alarm throbbed in her throat.

He froze. Tension pulled across his cheekbones. His nostrils twitched and his lips thinned against his teeth.

"Keep going," she pleaded. It hurt, but beneath the sting was a sweet stimulation that called to her.

He forged in, the pressure and stretch becoming insistent. Just when she thought she couldn't take it, his hips sealed themselves to hers. He let out a shaken breath and cupped his hand against the side of her head, one thumb playing at the corner of her mouth.

"All right?"

His throbbing flesh was inside her. She could feel him twitching within her in the most astonishing sensation. His hard legs kept hers open for his invasion and the rest of him was a heavy weight upon her.

In every way she was at his mercy. Helpless. But when he nibbled at the edge of her jaw and breathed, "You feel so good," she felt precious. Like she was giving him something merely by allowing this.

Her eyes stung then and he noticed the dampness gathering there. His brows came together. "Hurt?"

"A little. It's okay, it's just..." She almost said

"big." *Not that, Ilona. He'll laugh.* "I didn't know it would feel like this. It's just sex. Everyone does it." But it was overwhelming.

A shadow might have passed within his arousal-fogged gaze, but he touched his mouth to hers and murmured, "No one does it like this. We're special. Move when you're ready. Find out what you like."

Curious, she shifted a little, arched and rubbed. Little fires restarted within her. An enticing promise called to her, keeping her searching for those sparks and swirls of pleasure. Her sensitized skin grew a fresh batch of goose bumps and her hands *required* knowledge of his back and shoulders and buttocks. Her mouth sought each place she could reach, opening against his upper arm and throat and chin, learning his textures and taste.

As she moved her hips, she discovered pressure and stimulation in some places that overcame the sting in others. In fact, when her knees bent against his hips, he slid a fraction deeper and the nudge of his pubic bone grinding against her mound brought a fresh spark of need to where they were joined.

She instinctually found a rhythm that built

those deep, delicious sensations and realized after a moment that he was moving with her in this dance, meeting and matching her movements with perfect synchronicity. It was beautiful, really.

It was lovemaking. This was how it happened. She clung to the source of her pleasure—him and his flesh and the dream that they were one. He moved with more power, withdrawing and returning, reinforcing that he was strong enough to hurt her, but was taking care not to. He delivered that exquisite sting and the fiery ache that was becoming essential and she welcomed it. Welcomed him. *Come back come back. Again, again, again.*

She bit her lip and moaned with abandon, completely immersed in the ecstasy his body inflicted on hers. She surrendered to it. Surrendered to him and his ragged breaths and the way he caught a hand under her tailbone and tilted her hips and drove even deeper.

There it was, the pinnacle bathed in light and the chasm beyond.

This was how love happened. In this moment of joy and trust and feeling deeply attuned. Right here, she believed Leander had the power to make everything right in her world. She believed he would be bound to her always and she would never be alone again.

In this moment, as another climax swept up to suffuse her, her heart opened to let him in. She felt her love for him encompass her and believed he loved her back.

He must. He was shouting her name and they were tumbling through the unknown together, knitted and knotted and *one*.

It would be hours before she saw sex as the false promise it really was.

CHAPTER TWELVE

"YOU'VE MISTAKEN ME for someone who forgives easily. I'm not," were Leander's last words before he closed her into her car in the underground parking lot of the penthouse.

Ilona sputtered with laughter, besotted as she turned her head to watch him while her car pulled away and he moved across to his own. She was giddy with sex hormones and wedding excitement and stupid, cupid love. She closed her eyes as she came into the light, holding onto the image of his stern, unsmiling profile, adoring him.

At the rehearsal dinner last night, Susan had cornered Leander into picking her up this morning to bring her to the wedding, suggesting he breakfast with her since Ilona was going to the house early, meeting the team who would help her dress.

You're not supposed to see your bride until

the wedding anyway. It's bad luck, Susan had scolded him.

They still hadn't told anyone they were already married. They were also the only ones who knew they had consummated that marriage. Three torrid times. Those memories from yesterday afternoon, from last night before they fell asleep, then again this morning were delicious secrets Ilona held close inside herself where they warmed her all the way until she arrived at the house.

Feodor met her, already run off his feet. "The WiFi is spotty and of course the florist hasn't arrived yet," he muttered. "Hercules texted best wishes and said he's still willing to give you away."

If things had been different, she might have asked him to.

"Tell him Leander's mother will walk me up the aisle." Originally, she and Leander had planned to walk in together, but Susan had asked for the honor last night. Ilona couldn't refuse her, not when it made her feel as though she was being accepted into his life.

She went upstairs where she spent the next two hours being primped and pampered and polished. When her makeup was flawless and flowers intricately woven into her gathered locks and she had nibbled enough of an omelet to tide her over through the next hours, she was laced into her gown.

It was fitted through the bodice and hips then flared midthigh. Its long bell sleeves were made of pure lace. Diamanté crystals were strategically woven throughout to create flashes of rainbow brilliance. Like the sleeves, her back was bare skin beneath fine, netted lace with delicate floral patterns and two dozen tiny pearl buttons down her spine.

She felt more beautiful than she ever had in her life.

What would Leander think, she wondered?

"Is Leander here?" she asked. The sound of musicians tuning their instruments had become soothing background melodies while the din of gathering voices had grown.

"He might be having trouble getting in," someone said. "The drive is clogged by cars dropping guests."

"I suppose," Ilona said, but her stomach curdled.

Midas, she thought. If anything went wrong

today, he would be to blame. But for some reason, her mind went back to what Leander had said as they had parted this morning.

You've mistaken me for someone who forgives easily.

She had thought he meant he wasn't prepared to forgive his mother.

Now, as she moved so she could see the growing crowd assembling on the lawn, she wondered if he had meant her. A Pagonis.

Her stomach cramped again.

Two hundred people had been invited. They spilled onto the grounds, eating hors d'oeuvres and drinking champagne, waiting to convene in the rows of chairs on either side of the white-carpeted aisle before an arbor that had been built for the occasion.

He already married me, she reassured herself. There would be no point in leaving her at the altar.

Except to humiliate her.

Her stomach kept taking dizzying swoops of grim premonition.

"Ilona?" Feodor came into the lounge where she was hovering. He looked pale. Two men stood behind him, both wearing police uniforms.

Her heart nearly came out her throat. "Is Leander here?" she asked, hearing the desperation in her own voice.

"No. And, um…"

"Ilona Callas?" One man introduced himself as a lieutenant inspector. "You have to come with us. You're under arrest for trafficking narcotics."

Midas has done this. That's what Ilona told herself for the first two hours, while she waited for her lawyer to appear.

The police hadn't even let her change from her gown. They had put her in handcuffs and forced her to endure the humiliation of being loaded into their car before the shocked audience of her wedding guests.

Then she was left in a cell with two other women who were less extravagantly dressed, but equally miserable and quietly distressed.

Her flustered lawyer appeared, mumbling about unforeseen delays before he explained that the police had received evidence that drugs were being smuggled in shipments from Callas Cosmetics. Ilona had been implicated by a photo and a signature.

"That's doctored evidence!" she cried.

"It's flimsy, I know," her lawyer said grimly. "It's not even due process. The police have forty-eight hours to make an arrest without a warrant if they catch someone in the act of commiting a crime. They're claiming they had to act because you're about to leave on your honeymoon. I'll be filing for a dismissal and they will eventually face a disciplinary investigation, but that doesn't help you in this moment. I have to secure your release through normal channels which will take time. Hours. Not days," he assured her, but she was losing heart by the minute.

"Has..." She was afraid to ask, afraid of the answer. "Has Leander been informed?" *Why isn't he here?*

"He's not answering his phone and—" Her lawyer's face tightened. "There's a report his yacht left port with him on it."

You've mistaken me for someone who forgives easily.

If there had been anything substantial in her stomach, she would have thrown it up.

"It shouldn't be much longer," her lawyer promised and she was shown back to her cell.

When she was finally released, it was because her bail had been posted by Hercules. She went home with him.

A woman's startled cry opened Leander's eyes, but nothing about what he saw made sense. Was that a bed leg? Why was he drunk? *Where was he?*

"Help, help!" the woman cried.

"Is he dead?" another voice asked with alarm.

"I don't know."

They sounded like they were in another room. He heard the rush of feet coming toward him and pushed himself up enough to prop his back on the side of the mattress.

Was that his mother on the bed? He reached for her wrist and she moaned slightly, twitching. Alive, at least. *What the hell had happened?*

He swore, recalling helping her to the bed because she had suddenly felt ill. One minute they'd been sharing coffee, the next they'd both been nauseous and dizzy. Leander had staggered her to the bed and…must have blacked out because he couldn't remember anything after that.

"I was drugged," he told the women in housekeeping uniforms, both blinking with astonishment at him. It was the only explanation. "What time is it?"

He turned his head to the clock on the nightstand and swore again. *The wedding.*

"Ilona." Her name was a bitter pang of regret in the back of his throat.

He patted his jacket until he found his phone. Another string of curses came out of him as he saw dozens of texts and attempts to call, most of them from Androu, but others, too. His lawyer, guests from the wedding. All were asking some version of, Where are you? What do you want me to do?

"Get my mother a doctor," he said to the housekeeper as he forced himself onto his feet. His whole body felt a thousand times heavier than it should.

"Did I miss the wedding?" his mother asked on a sob of anguish. "I didn't mean to let her down. I swear, Leander." Tears dampened her fluttering lashes.

He squeezed her hand. "It's not your fault."

It was his. "But I have to find Ilona. A doctor is coming," he promised and dialed Dino as he bounced off the door frame into the hall. "Bring the car around."

"I'm having new tires put on. I stepped away for a cigarette and they were all slashed."

Of course they were. Leander could have smashed his phone to pieces at that moment, he was so furious. He ended his call and hit the speed dial for Androu.

"Finally!" Androu said in a choked voice. "I couldn't reach you—"

"Is she okay? Hurt?" His heart was clenched into a hard fist inside his chest. "Where is she?"

A beat of surprise, then, "Still with her brother, I think."

"Midas?" Again, he nearly battered his phone to pieces on the elevator wall. Had she somehow been part of this? Tricking him into going to his mother and risking both their lives with whatever sedative had been slipped into their food?

"The other one," Androu said. "I think. Feodor stopped responding to my texts, but the last I heard, Hercules was bailing her out."

"She was *arrested*?"

* * *

Hercules had brought her a clean set of clothes to change into—men's drawstring pants and a T-shirt that was likely tight on him and hung loose on her. Ilona changed into them for the drive to his place where he made her one of his fancy coffees from his espresso maker.

He took his phone into his bedroom when Odessa began ranting over video chat about the scandal Ilona had brought to the family name today.

Ilona could still hear both sides of the conversation. Hercules occupied an upper-level floor of an industrial building. His bedroom was behind a partition made of glass cubes. The only door in the place was on the toilet. The rest was open concept with easels and canvases before the tall windows. Brushes and rags were littered everywhere, all emitting the chemical scent of paint and turpentine.

When there was a buzz for the service elevator, Ilona reached to press the button, but paused. Feodor was bringing her phone and purse, but she had been burned too many times lately.

She opened the call to the speaker below. "Feodor?"

"It's me," Leander said. "Midas drugged me. I just woke up."

"I don't care."

"What do you mean you don't care?" he thundered. "I would have been there, Ilona. I wouldn't have let that happen to you."

"But you *did*." For the first time since the cold handcuffs had encircled her wrists, her eyes grew hot and her throat began to ache with a pressure she wasn't sure she could withstand. "I told you I didn't want to be in the middle of this war of yours. I told you I didn't want to trust you because you would only let me down."

"I'm here now. *Let me up*."

"Don't," Hercules said, appearing from behind the partition.

"Is she there with you?" Odessa cried.

"Don't tell Midas," Hercules warned his mother, but they both knew she absolutely would.

The threat of having to face Midas was horrible enough Ilona knew she had to leave. She pressed the button to allow Leander up.

Hercules told Odessa he would call her back, then glared at Ilona. "Why did you do that?"

She didn't get a chance to reply. Leander appeared in the cage of the elevator like an angry god. He raked back the grill with a clatter, stepped in, then halted to stare at her.

She didn't move, but the shock was wearing off and hatred was seeping in to take its place.

"Get the hell out," Hercules told him. "Leave her alone."

"You're the hero now? When you're letting your brother assault her and manufacture drug charges against her? You and I will settle our differences in due course. Right now, I'm taking Ilona home."

"*You* think you're on the high ground?" Hercules scoffed. "You only tried to marry her to get your hands on our company! Do you realize that, Ilona?"

Leander transferred his sharp gaze from Hercules to her. "You haven't told him?"

"Told me what?"

"I'm too ashamed," Ilona said, purely out of malice.

Leander flinched and she immediately felt

small, but Leander told Hercules, "We're already married."

"Ilona," Hercules breathed in horror. "You didn't."

"Tell your brother his attempt to stop our wedding didn't work. Let him know that investigators are already looking for the attendant who poisoned my mother and me as well as any connection he has to Ilona's arrest. You should be asking yourself how much longer you're willing to cover for him because I am very, very angry and I will not stop until *everyone* who played a part in this is extremely sorry."

"I—" Hercules was shooting his gaze back and forth between them, the helplessness in him breaking her heart. He was still there on the inside, caring for her, but not enough. Not even enough to save himself.

"Come." Leander's voice gentled as he crouched beside her. "I promised I would take you away from them and I will."

Leander had been blind with rage since leaving the hotel, but he had arrived below as Feodor was stepping from Ilona's car, her bag and other belongings in hand.

"Wait here," Leander had ordered the PA. "We won't be long."

Feodor had tried to stare him down and Leander had spared one moment to appreciate the man's loyalty to Ilona, but Leander was collecting his wife and that was that.

He physically gathered her up, ignoring her half-hearted attempt to be set on her feet.

"I don't want to go home with you," she said, voice filled with the ache of her disappointment in him.

"The yacht is waiting." To take them on their honeymoon. He'd been looking forward to it and she seemed to have been, too. Before.

What a bloody mess.

"They said it was gone. That you *left*."

He could hear the knife that had been to her heart. He paused to absorb how badly he'd failed her today. He hated failure. *Hated it.*

"That was a lie told to distress you." It had worked. She was insubstantial in his arms. The corners of her mouth dragged down, her sadness profound enough to send a fracture across his chest. "Do you have anything here that you want to take?"

"No."

Hercules turned his head, sending Leander's gaze into the corner. Her wedding gown was draped over a chair, it's white layers like a snowdrift blown into a corner, but the kind that had weathered winter and was melting in spring, streaked by dirt and stains, no longer pure and pretty.

She had been excited to wear that gown. Leander had seen it when she had told his mother about it. He was so sorry in that moment. So sorry that all his precautions had been against infiltrators and criminals. No one was supposed to be able to get to her today. It hadn't occurred to him that Midas would send the *police* after her.

With one final look of contempt toward Hercules, he made the lethal promise, "I'll see you at the next board meeting."

CHAPTER THIRTEEN

ILONA WOKE TO DARKNESS, eyes and throat still raw from the storm of tears that had taken her once she had come aboard the yacht. She had cried and shouted and said awful things to Leander.

"I *hate* you," she had screamed. The words had rasped from the very depth of her being.

"I know."

He hadn't offered any excuses. He hadn't reminded her that he'd been unconscious the whole time. *He* wasn't the one who had set her up to be arrested, but he had let her berate him as though he was.

It wasn't him she hated. It wasn't him she wanted to shout at, but he took it and held her when she fell apart. He tucked her into bed when she was reduced to a few stray sniffles and a desire to forget everything in the amnesia of sleep.

And now he rolled toward her in the bed and

rubbed her arm. "Shhh. You're safe. Go back to sleep."

She couldn't, not until she said, "I'm sorry."

"Don't." His hand paused to squeeze. "I knew he would try to disrupt the wedding, but your bodyguards couldn't stop actual police. I expected an attack on *me*, not my mother."

"I'm apologizing for making you think that I blame you. I don't. It's not your fault that he's a terrible human being."

"But I should have expected—"

"Leander." She slithered near and something eased in her when he adjusted his position and gathered her close, aligned along his front. It was deeply reassuring and everything she needed when she felt so disjointed and broken.

"We agreed that he doesn't come to bed with us," she reminded.

His chest expanded and she thought he was about to argue, but he only let out his breath in a resigned sigh.

"All right. We'll talk in the morning. Good night." He pressed a kiss to her forehead.

She was still wearing Hercules's clothes, but Leander wore only briefs. She slid her hands across the warm planes of his body, rubbing her feet on the tops of his.

"Angele mou." He caught her hand.

"You don't want to kiss and make up?" She extracted her hand and caressed his shape through his briefs. Squeezed in the way that made his breath hiss. "It feels like you do."

He laughed softly and his nose bumped her cheek. His mouth found the corner of hers. "If it will make you feel better, then yes. I do." He was smiling; she could feel it.

"You'll make that great sacrifice for me?" This too was love, she realized, as softness and light crept back into her, edging out the day's darkness of anguish and resentment. It was soft caresses in the night, quiet words and help removing her clothes. It was tenderness and forgiveness and being both hurried, yet not, kissing and caressing and building something beyond tension and arousal. Trust and care and *need*.

They both gasped as he thrust into her and he held her tight, saying against her ear, "I thought I might never feel you like this again. Your lips still taste of salt."

From her tears. But his kiss dissolved those

lingering traces and they moved and rolled and made so much love. When he brought her atop him, she threw off the blankets and straddled him and ran her hands over his chest, thinking, *I love you. I love you.*

"Ilona." He cupped her head and brought her down for a long kiss. Then he rolled her beneath him again, thrusting and thrusting until she was lost to a long, intense orgasm.

His teeth scraped her chin and he coaxed, "Again."

And that was how the night passed, in a blur of connection and closeness and endless pleasure.

I love you. I love you.

Did she realize she had said it aloud? If she did, was she wondering why he hadn't said it in return? Had she even been telling the truth? How could she love him when he'd failed her so spectacularly?

He didn't even know what love was. Not really. Oh, he had loved his parents as a child, but his mother had broken his heart and his father had been, well, a functioning adult, but there had been a certain amount of parenting the parent in their relationship.

To Leander's mind, love was responsibility. It was duty. It was suffering rejection and accepting their failings. Of missing them and not being there when they had needed him most. Love was intertwined with inadequacy and loss.

Even his most recent conversation with his mother, when they had unknowingly shared her laced coffee, had left him tasting the bitterness of being in the wrong. She had reminded him of the times she had invited him to come for Christmas and other events. *Come see my show.*

His father had always grown too anxious over his impending departure. Leander was the one who had canceled and stayed home, but he'd been a child, oblivious to what he was doing to her and their relationship. Oblivious to how limited time really was.

So, to have Ilona's love was to feel a weight on him. But when he looked on her as she came to the rail at the bow, her expression glowing with delight, the weight was only that of a little bird on his heart. An iridescent hummingbird that zoomed in, piercing into his tenderest flesh with her tiny claws.

"That's Paxos! How did you know?" She beamed up at him.

"How do you think? I asked Feodor where he thought you would most like to go. I don't think he'll be so forthcoming in future. Do you know if he's speaking to Androu yet?"

"Leander." She touched her chest in mock shock. "Are you matchmaking?" She accompanied her accusation with a skim of her fingers down his spine.

Her touch might as well be a bell pull, tugging and ringing all his nerve endings to life despite the fact they'd only left their wrecked bed an hour ago.

"Hardly. Our PAs need to communicate." He scooped her under his arm and gave her a squeeze. "How else will I know where to meet you for lunch?"

"Issue them a memo explaining the benefits of kissing and making up," she suggested with a bat of her lashes at him.

"You're in a cheeky mood." He liked it.

"I'm floating up there somewhere." She waved at the cloudless sky above the island of her birth, then wrapped both her arms around his waist, gazing up at him with eyes of inky wonder. "You brought me *home*."

The emotion in her voice sent a piercing sensation into his throat and vibrations rolled in his chest like thunder. Pride, he thought with irony. He was pleased he had given her something that made her smile so unreservedly, but there was also humility in how little it took to please her.

"You're not wishing I'd taken you to Paris for shopping?"

"Oh, I'll be shopping," she assured him. "This small island can't produce enough soap and olive oil for Callas, but I order for my own use several times a year. The fragrances are pure nostalgia triggers."

Her elation was so beautiful, she stole his breath.

Her resilience awed him, actually. He didn't know how she was so good at catching at a moment like this, of grasping the happiness and erasing everything else. His anger was still a cold wraith inside him, swirling and darkening his vision even as the affectionate way she rested her head on his chest filled him with softness and light.

He wouldn't spoil her mood, though. He rubbed her arm and kissed her temple and said, "I need to make one call, then we'll jump on the tender and go ashore."

His one call was to Androu. He issued a dozen orders, some to release his various hounds against Midas. Others were PR related, countering the headlines about Ilona's arrest. Each time Leander saw the photos of her being arrested in her wedding gown, he tasted blood. Midas would pay for that if it was the last thing he ever did.

"Your mother is safely on her way home," Androu informed him as they wrapped up. "Once the hotel identified him, the room service attendant turned himself in. He claims he only meant to drug your mother, not you. It was meant to draw you from the wedding to her side. He gave up the name of the intermediary who hired him. Investigators are trying to tie him to Midas. They *have* found a connection between one of the arresting inspectors and Midas."

Leander fought back a rush of *I knew it* rage.

"Keep me informed. And…" Was he losing his edge? "If you need me to speak to Feodor, to explain that you weren't to blame for my absence yesterday, I can do that."

There was such a lengthy silence, Leander thought the connection had been lost.

Then, "Thank you, but we're both professionals. Any personal issues will be handled between us and won't affect our work."

That wasn't entirely what Leander was worried about. He appreciated both men. Androu had put out a thousand fires while trying to find Leander yesterday. Feodor would die for Ilona. They were too valuable to lose, but Leander didn't want either of them to be uncomfortable in their work life.

He *was* losing his edge, growing invested in the private lives of not only his own employee, but his wife's.

He donned his usual air of detachment and ended the call, heading outside to take Ilona to shore.

Paxos was a bustling tourist destination in the high season, as all Greek islands were, but it was inconvenient enough to reach that it wasn't as overrun as most others. Antipaxos, its smaller, modest sister, was even more serene, especially now as they explored the pair of islands in the waning shoulder season.

For the first few days, they sailed between Gaios, Loggos and Lakka, walking the narrow streets of each, stopping for iced coffee, eating in the main square and poking in shops for small treasures. When they reached the isolated west side, they went ashore to visit hidden coves and empty beaches and swam into the famed blue caves.

"I've always wanted to do this," Ilona said as they were treading water in one cool, shadowy cave, the water glowing dark blue around them. Her hushed voice echoed off the dripping ceiling.

"Why haven't you?" Leander asked.

"Fear." It was still there, but she was beginning to see that it was in her power to decide how much power that emotion had over her.

For instance, she kept holding back the words, those terrifyingly revealing words that were on her tongue and in her throat and pulsing in her heart every moment she was near him.

Why didn't she want to say them? Fear. Fear

that he would reject her. Fear that he wouldn't feel the same. Fear that speaking her love aloud would break a spell and change all that was good between them.

But how he reacted was not in her control. If he didn't feel the same, that was his loss. She would rather allow her love to imbue her whole soul and flow freely from her heart than keep it boxed and dammed and compressed inside her like a miser hoarding gold.

"I love you, you know," she told him, and as she did, a glorious weight lifted off her. She became part of the air and salt and water, buoyant and whole. Universal.

"I do know," he said gravely. "I never want to hurt you. I hope you know that."

It did hurt to hear him say that, but the hurt was for him, for his inability to release himself to this thing that was expansive and healing and terrifying, yet so very right.

With a sway of her arms and a low, lazy kick, she moved across to him. He caught her and cradled her, holding her up as she wound her legs around his waist and cupped his jaw in her wet hands.

"Don't look at me with regret," she scolded

gently. "Not ever. You've given me things I never thought I'd have. Courage." Her smile wobbled with self-deprecation. "Freedom." And maybe…

The timing was wrong. Her cycle was due in a day or two. She wouldn't get her hopes up, but maybe, someday, he would give her love in its purest form.

"I don't ever want you to be afraid again. But I'm afraid for you when you're this unguarded. I will protect you in every way I can, Ilona, but I need you to protect yourself. Even from me. Especially from me. Can you do that?"

"No. It's too late," she said wryly and tried to kiss him.

He balked briefly, then kissed her back. Hard. As if he couldn't help himself. As if she was the source of his oxygen.

Then he drew back and released her completely. The seawater felt cold against skin that had been warmed by his body. His shadowed profile searched the darkest corners of the cave.

"We can't make love here," she said. "We might get crabs."

His crack of laughter bounced off the ceiling.

"True." He shook his head at her, then sobered. "That's not what I was looking for."

She knew. He was looking for some way to let her down easy or put distance between them. He didn't want to hurt her, but he wanted to protect himself. She understood that. All too well.

"I've had to take care of myself for a long time, Leander. I know how." She dipped under and swam toward the sunlight, surfacing to say, "Let's go back to the yacht. I'm hungry."

Leander felt trapped in one of those medieval devices, the kind that was attempting to tear him apart.

One half of himself was firmly affixed in the heaven that was his wife. They made love and shared inside jokes and talked of what they wanted to accomplish in the future. She was fascinating in her approach to her work, smart and ambitious, yet driven by empathy and a desire to make the world a better place. If she wasn't so devoted to her own business, he would have lured her to a lead position in his own.

The other part of him was dragged down by

the grim hatred and thirst for revenge that had governed his life for so long. He couldn't forget that soiled wedding gown or her absolute loss of faith in him. He *had* to make good on his promise to avenge her. It was as important to him as righting the wrong his father had suffered.

Leander began making headway once he was no longer giving in to the lazy bliss of sailing and lovemaking. They returned to Athens where they both became busy with work demands and, as Ilona had predicted that long-ago day, with social obligations. For some reason, being married meant invitations had increased exponentially.

Perhaps it was their notoriety. The headlines after the ruined wedding had shouted, Married in Secret! False Arrest Fails to Halt True Love, and More Family Twists than a Greek Tragedy.

The stock value in Pagonis had dropped shortly after, when an enterprising reporter, aided by Leander, had dug up his father's original lawsuit over the stolen technology. Midas disappeared from the public eye once he was identified by someone in Ilona's building from the night he had attacked her. He was quietly divesting some of his lesser, overseas proper-ties, likely to pay his PR and legal teams.

Leander doubled the security presence that dogged him and Ilona. It was inconvenient, but he was especially concerned when she was at work.

"Half a floor may come open in my build-ing," he told her one morning. He was actually considering not renewing the existing lease to vacate it. "You could move your headquarters there, leave the lab to do its work where it is."

"And meet you in a broom closet during coffee break?" she teased. "Delightful as that sounds, I'm in the middle of restructuring. Now that I have full control, I want to be on-site."

He didn't love that answer, but he let it drop since they were arriving at tonight's gala and always caused a stir when they walked a carpet.

Leander liked to believe it was because Ilona had finally embraced all that she'd naturally been given. She was an absolute vision wher-ever she went. Tonight, she wore a figure-hug-ging black gown with intricate silver beading decorating its waist and hem. The feature that had him biting his lip, however, was the sleeve-less style that lovingly accentuated the fullness of her breasts. The way three very thin straps ran down her otherwise naked back made him want to keep her in this car and kiss every inch of skin he could find.

But he helped her rise and offered a steady arm as they made their way toward the entrance of the hotel.

"Who are you wearing? Tell us about your gown!" photographers shouted.

Ilona always paused to tell them, having accepted her infamy. In fact, she had turned it into a strength when these hounds had made their first appearance after their honeymoon. Facing a gauntlet of paparazzi and speculation, she had answered the question about her gown, then joked, "I wanted to look my best, in case I'm arrested again."

"Look your best for your arrest" had become a meme overnight and was regularly pasted over her photo in whichever glamorous gown was her latest. Anticipation and mystique had grown over what she would wear next, the furor so intense that top designers were now sending her gowns in hopes of gaining exposure.

This evening would have been yet another rousing success if two things hadn't happened.

The first was that Odessa was intending to be here. Leander had learned she was on the guest list and would have had her removed—or would have refused to attend—but Ilona pushed his concerns aside.

"We have to cross paths at some point."

Leander still would have kept Ilona on the far side of the ballroom, but it happened that Odessa came onto the dance floor as he was circling with Ilona. It was a deliberate ambush, he suspected, since Odessa spoke loud enough to turn heads.

"That slut."

Leander instinctually angled his body to shield Ilona while glaring a warning at the woman, but Ilona brushed him off and turned to confront her stepmother.

"You raised three children, Odessa. At least one of them turned out very poorly. Any blame for that child's behavior lies with you."

An amused murmur went through the crowd and someone guffawed. Leander was pretty damned impressed himself.

"Would you excuse me?" Ilona asked Leander and disappeared to the powder room.

He waited near the entrance for her return to

the ballroom, worried the confrontation had taken more out of her than she had let on, especially when she appeared only to say she would rather leave.

"I should have told them to remove her from the list," Leander said in the car.

"Hmm? Oh, I don't care about her." Ilona flicked her wrist in dismissal.

"But you're upset."

The corners of her mouth went down. "I had a backache earlier and hoped I was wrong, but… I'm not pregnant."

"Oh. I'm sorry." He was, but the words were stupidly inadequate, especially because this was the second time she was disappointed on that front. The first had been while they'd still been sailing. She'd been philosophical, saying the timing wasn't right, but this time he could see she was genuinely saddened.

So was he, more sharply than he expected, but he didn't say so. He reached for her instead, drawing her across and into his lap.

But as he held her, the ache of something lost or a chance missed became so unbearable, he did what he always did, rather than dwell on the pain of everyday life. He turned his mind to his revenge.

The board meeting was two weeks away. Soon, he kept promising himself. All the pieces were coming together and soon he would swing his final death blow and everything would feel right again.

Ilona had begun to believe happily-ever-after was real and that she was living it.

After steeping in the harmony of their honeymoon, they had returned to Athens where she took full custody of her company. It was thrilling! No more Midas poking his nose in, questioning her decisions. She didn't even have to take his calls, not that he tried to reach out. He seemed preoccupied with keeping his name out of unfavorable headlines which suited her beautifully.

Ilona had half expected a call from Odessa after her performance at the gala the other night, but according to Feodor, Leander and Ilona were more coveted guests than Odessa was. The word was out that Odessa had seriously misbehaved. Her invitations had dried up overnight.

Ilona was neither pleased nor sorry. She was indifferent and that, too, was thrilling. She and Leander rarely spoke of any of that old, painful business. He had told her he was keeping a wall between her and his actions as a sort of protection against Midas retaliating, but she had actually started to believe they were both putting all of it behind them.

Not so, apparently.

"I had lunch with Hercules today," she told Leander with concern when they were sitting down for a rare dinner at home. She had served the meal the housekeeper had prepared and had sent the woman home early so they could have some privacy for their discussion.

"Why?" Leander's shoulders tensed and his voice became lethal.

"Because he invited me." She poured the wine because he was only sitting very still, staring at her through narrowed eyes. "Have you really stolen his entire show?"

"No." He picked up the glass she filled and took a healthy swallow. "I stalled it."

"Leander—"

"Do not defend him," he warned. "He has

benefited off my father's work, same as the rest of them. He has to pay."

"And he sees that. It's fair for you to go after his job at Pagonis. Go after the profits from his shares. But going after his paintings isn't right."

"Why not? How did he afford that studio and all the time and supplies to paint? Hmm?"

"The value isn't in the canvases and tubes of paint. It's what he did with it. He's an artist. A creator. What you're doing *hurts* him, Leander." Like her, Hercules didn't know how to be happy. He was afraid of it. But when it was only him and his brush, he poured out his soul. He had been in tears when he'd told Ilona what Leander had done.

"Good," Leander said flatly.

"Really? You have no empathy, no regard for him at all? He bailed me out of jail when you couldn't," she reminded.

"And remains complicit in all the things Midas has done to you," he shot back. "How can you accept that?"

"I'm not asking you to retaliate for *me*. Do you realize that? You deserve recompense for what Midas did. You do," she assured him. "But this...blind determination of yours to inflict pain is not healthy. Especially if you think you're doing it for my sake. I don't want you to do that, Leander. It makes you no better than Midas if you enjoy hurting people."

"I'm righting the scales of justice."

"No. What you're doing to Hercules is *punishment*." It was the twist in Leander's psyche she had feared could happen.

"You're really taking his side over ours?" He was more than affronted. Astounded.

"How is it 'our' side? You're not including me in any of this. Remember?" For her protection, he had said, but she suspected it was yet again a trust issue. She had been feeling so close to him. She *loved* him. But he was stuck in the past, still allowing Midas to dictate who he was and what he did and how he felt.

"Fine," he snapped. "It's not our side. It's mine. So pick which one you're on and it better be mine."

A tearing sensation went through her middle. She looked down at her fragrant lamb and roasted potato, appetite gone.

Tragically, she wasn't as surprised as she ought to be. She had always expected it could come to this. Leander was so fixated on his need for vengeance, he would push aside everything she offered him. Everything they'd made together.

But what had they made? If his revenge was still more important than she was, if it was his everything, then they didn't have anything.

"I know you can't see it, but I'm not fighting for Hercules. I'm fighting for you," she told him shakily, throat going tight. "For *us*."

"You're fighting *me*. You're asking me to give up."

"To give in. A *little*."

"No!" He rose and left the table so abruptly, the wine sloshed in their glasses. "And the fact you're pushing me on this makes me wonder if you've *ever* been on my side. Is all of this a smokescreen?" He waved at their house, the one that had begun to feel like a home. "Because it won't work. I won't let you derail me from seeing this through."

A searing line sat like a spear from her throat into her chest, holding her still as she absorbed how painful it was to watch him lose faith in her so completely. To question her love for him.

"Do you remember what I said I would do if things came down to you or me?" she asked, voice thick with the anguish spreading through her.

She heard him swallow, but she couldn't seem to raise her eyes to look at him. She couldn't bear to see how little he valued the heart she had given him.

"I'm not cutting you loose," he said through clenched teeth.

"You're asking me to look the other way while you hurt someone I care about."

"I thought you cared about *me*," he shot back ferociously. "I thought you *loved* me."

His bitter taunt was the final straw. She felt the break inside her, but she had always known he would break her heart. She hadn't known it would be an actual shattering sensation in her chest, the resulting pain exploding like a hive of wasps, all determined to sting her to death.

"I do love you. But you don't love me." She could survive that, she could. But, "It's obvious you don't even care enough to recognize that what you're asking me to do will damage something in me that won't be repaired. I can't be part of this blood feud any longer, Leander.

I can't side with you. For my own self-preservation, I have to side with *myself.*"

He let her go. She promised to keep her guard detail, but those were the last words they exchanged. She packed and hovered an extra minute, perhaps waiting for him to say more, to give in and beg her to stay, but he had nothing to say. He had come too far to give up now. How could she not see that?

He was furious with her. Forsaken. She had known who she was marrying! How could she desert him when he was on the cusp of vanquishing his enemy for good?

Hercules had come begging her to persuade him to show mercy. Odessa was rumored to be preparing for an extended stay in New York, having become deeply unpopular. Midas, that vile maggot of a man, was gasping for financial air. His reputation was tarnished, associated with Ilona's false arrest and other corrupt deeds. Leander hadn't leaked her restraining order for Midas to the press, but that too was being reported as an "unconfirmed rumor." Even the patent question on Leander's father's technology had been resurrected, proving Midas had feet of clay.

Leander *had* to seize his day when the board meeting arrived, but felt curiously flat when it did. He climbed into the back of his SUV, aware that he would push Midas off his pedestal once and for all today, but there was no excitement for the other man's downfall. All he could think about was Ilona.

Leander had already made enough compromises for her. Hadn't he? Did she not recall that he had agreed to run the company in good faith? Rather than level it? Why was that not enough for her? What more did she need to hear before she would stand behind him? Stand *beside* him?

God, her absence hurt. He had moved through these last days in a zombielike trance, making his final calls, ensuring the various board members would support him. They had all agreed to back his bid for the chair, but there was no satisfaction in it.

He, the man who had preferred for years to walk alone and eat alone and sleep alone was... alone. Desolate.

He couldn't stop thinking reliving those intimate moments when she had brightened and softened and exploded. Was it the sex? Did she not enjoy it the way he did? Because it nearly killed him in the most deliciously satisfying ways. Every time. She was fierce and uninhibited and they always seemed to arrive at culmination together, bodies shaking and hearts crashing and ecstatic cries filling the room.

He didn't want to lose that. How could she let it go so easily?

Was it his desire for children? The fact it hadn't happened? Did she blame him?

Was it *him*?

Here was the deepest bruise, the darkest fear, the rawest worry. Was there some flaw in himself that he didn't see? One that caused the people he loved to disappear when he needed them most?

Oh, hell. He closed his eyes and the breath he sucked in seemed filled with powdered glass, expanding in his lungs with fiery tingles, leaving him without oxygen. Lightheaded.

He loved her.

The poignant arrow of love was lodged so deeply in his heart, it had become a part of him without his realizing it. He loved her. He loved her beyond what he thought was possible. Beyond what any one person had felt for another in the history of time. His love was epic and terrifying and so bright and *right*, it caused a hot pressure behind his eyes and in his throat.

That's why his chest was a hollow, cavernous, windy space. That's why his bed was, too. And their new home. Ilona could have moved into her unused bedroom, but instead she had left him completely. He couldn't bear it. Not for another second.

He turned his head. "Call Feodor and find out where she's staying."

Androu didn't ask who he meant. He placed the call and his mouth went flat. "Feodor can't say," he relayed.

"Give me that," Leander snarled, holding out his palm. "Tell me where she is, Feodor." He *needed* her.

"I genuinely don't know. I swear. She asked me to get our new CEO organized—"

"Your new—? She stepped down from running Callas?" Leander sat up and clamped a hand on Dino's shoulder, ensuring his driver knew a sudden change in route might be necessary. "Is she even in Athens? Is she *accounted for*?"

"She texted twenty minutes ago, reminding me the plant in her office shouldn't be overwatered."

A ridiculously innocuous message, yet jealousy overwhelmed him that she continued to communicate with Feodor and wanted nothing to do with him. Because he had hurt her. He had asked her to compromise her principles to prove her love, which wasn't love at all.

He handed the phone back to Androu and stared at the back of Dino's head.

"She's on Paxos. She must be," Leander muttered.

"Would you...like me to have the yacht prepared?" Androu asked tentatively.

Dino was looking at him in the rearview mirror. Both were awaiting his decision.

The helicopter would be faster, but what if she wasn't there? What if he went all that way and missed this meeting only to miss her?

Or worse, what if she was there and he went all that way only to have his love thrown back in his face?

He pinched the bridge of his nose, head tilted

back, filled with despair because he was about
to get everything he wanted—

No. He had *had* everything he wanted. Everything he needed. Ilona filled his life with meaning. She made him laugh, made every moment
of every day more enjoyable. She consistently
took him to the heights of profound pleasure.
She made him *happy.*

She made all that had happened in his past
bearable. She pushed it into the past so he could
look forward to his future with her.

Yet here he was, chasing destruction. Returning to the rotten tooth, rather than pulling it.
He was reveling in pain and wanted to inflict
it on others, purely to satisfy some demon inside him. He *was* no better than Midas.

"Dino—" he started to say, but Dino was
halting at the curb outside the Pagonis International building, the citadel Leander had spent
half a lifetime plotting to conquer.

How had he thought crushing someone would
fill the void inside him? Ilona filled that void.
Love did.

"Sir—" Androu was looking toward the
building.

"Find out if she's on Paxos," he told Androu without moving. "Ready the helicopter if she is."

"She's, um, here." Androu pushed from the vehicle and pointed. "I can see her through the window, looking at us." He lifted his hand in a wave.

Leander thrust himself from the car, heart following a second later and crashing into its place inside his chest, then filling his throat with a hammering pulse.

There she was, standing at the lobby window, solemn as she looked at him. Her hair was gathered in a single dark line against the front of her fitted navy blue dress. Always so beautiful and patient.

Patient enough to wait for a man who hadn't seen what he had? Was he too late to tell her how he felt?

Her expression didn't change as he strode into the building, but she turned to face him as he approached her.

"You're here." He opened his hands, wanting to grab her close. Wanting to *hold* her. Claim her. He wanted to kneel and beg her to never leave him again.

Her grave expression held him off. Her words about a blood feud were still ringing in his head.

"You don't have to be," he told her. "*We* don't have to be here. We can go anywhere."

Her eyes flared wider briefly before she said, "No. This is important. To both of us."

"*You* are important to me." He stepped forward and caught her cold hands. "I was going to come find you. Were you on Paxos?"

"I was, but—" Her face flexed with conflict, then her expression darkened as she looked past him.

Leander looked over his shoulder in time to see Midas pause as he spotted them. His face twisted and he continued on into the elevators.

Leander closed his hand more securely over Ilona's and felt her nails dig into his skin. When he looked at her, she wasn't showing signs of fear. Only anger. Steely determination.

"Let's go up," she said.

"You're sure?"

She nodded.

His heart lifted. He really was getting all he'd ever wanted.

They rose to the executive floor where the board of directors was assembling. As they entered, Leander overheard Midas arguing with Hercules.

"*I* vote Mother's share when she's out of town."

"Not this time." Hercules handed a piece of paper to someone stationed behind a laptop. "She gave me her proxy last night."

Midas narrowed his eyes. "Don't do anything stupid, Hercules. And why is *he* here, if you are?" Midas demanded as he transferred his glower to Ilona.

"Leander is my proxy. I'm here for other reasons," Ilona said with unruffled composure.

"She's a material witness," Leander clarified.

"To *what*? She's the one who was recently arrested. Not me."

"To the fact you're unfit to run Pagonis International," Leander said firmly. "Is everyone here? If so, I've added a leadership review to the top of the agenda."

"You're not in charge," Midas said. "So pipe down and get lost."

"I'm about to be in charge," Leander assured him, still holding Ilona's hand tight in his own. "Ladies and gentlemen, your current president is not only a walking disgrace, he'll soon be arrested on charges of assault and making false reports to the police. The things you've read online are not a PR smear as he would like you to believe. They're true and I've brought a presentation and documents to prove it." He nodded at Androu to start the projector.

"And embezzlement," Ilona interjected.

The room went silent. Everyone swiveled their attention to her. If a pin had dropped on the carpet, it would have struck with the force of a gong.

"That doesn't surprise me," Leander said to her. "But I don't have evidence of that. Do you?"

Midas snorted. "No. Because it's not true."

"I went to Paxos," she said. "I tried to buy the restaurant my mother once worked at, but learned it was already a Pagonis property. The proceeds are supposed to accrue for my use, but somehow the funds have been going into an account that eventually benefits Midas. And it's *empty.*"

All the heads swung back to Midas.

"Accounting error," he said with an unbothered blink. "I'm sure we can clear that up."

"Indeed. A full audit will be my first priority," Leander said with deadly assurance.

"You don't have the votes to take over," Midas said with a scathing chuckle. "I *know* you don't." He sent a glare of intimidation around the table.

Several people dropped their gazes and shifted in their seats.

"Did dear Mitéra instruct you to vote for him? Or me?" Midas asked Hercules as if he already knew the answer.

"She wanted me to vote for you," Hercules admitted then sent a glance toward Ilona as though looking for her reaction to that.

Midas sat back, releasing a snort that said, *See?*

"Until I explained that I spoke to the police and reported *I* was with her the night Ilona was assaulted in her apartment. And that you weren't with us." Hercules darted a glance at the gathering thunder in his brother's expression. He slouched protectively, but continued. "Once she realized she might be charged with providing a false alibi, she told me to vote with my conscience and left for New York. She'll remain there indefinitely."

Leander lifted a brow at Midas. *Your move.*

Midas ground his teeth so hard there should have been an audible crack. "That doesn't prove I was anywhere near Ilona."

"No," Ilona agreed with quiet dignity. "But the florist receipt for the roses and vase does imply you had them brought to my door. And my neighbor heard your voice. He and his partner both reported that I said it was you outside the door."

"Why are you still here?" Midas demanded hotly. "Only one of you should be in this room. You said he's here to vote your share so get out."

"The one who is leaving is you," Leander said with grim satisfaction. "Let's proceed with the vote."

Leander looked around the table, ending with Hercules. He felt a pinch of guilt for stalling the man's gallery showing. He had meant it to be further pressure against Midas, but Ilona was right. It had taken on a more personal element that wasn't right.

"Are you prepared to support me?" Leander asked, accepting that Hercules might refuse.

Hercules licked his lips and looked to Ilona

again. "I can't. Keep my paintings. Get whatever you can for them. Ilona has explained you're due compensation from our family. Let that be mine to you."

Leander didn't want *paintings*.

"Forget what ought to come to me," he said impatiently. "Are you really not prepared to depose the man who is responsible for all of these scandals? For harming your *sister*?" Leander shook his head in disbelief. Outrage. "I'm not here for payback." Not anymore. "He has to be stopped. Surely you can see that! I do have the votes, by the way," he told Midas as the other man made a dismissive noise. "Even without Hercules or your mother."

This time, however, when Leander looked around for confirmation, gazes dropped. Men and women he had spoken to himself, people who had assured him he had their support, couldn't meet his eyes.

A cold fist wrapped itself around his heart when even Rideaux winced and opened his mouth, seeming to search for words as he looked to Ilona.

"Leander." Her voice was apologetic, her touch on his arm light. Tentative.

And he knew. He knew that she had interfered. She was preventing him from taking over. She was *stealing* his moment when he should be exacting the revenge he had poured his heart and soul and blood and sweat into achieving.

She had warned him from the beginning she wouldn't be used as a pawn.

Apparently, she would rather be a queen.

Ilona had gone to Paxos determined to flip the script on her life. For most of her life, the dream of starting over there had been her mental refuge from heartache, the place she believed would be there for her when existence became too much to bear.

Leaving Leander had been excruciating, but staying hadn't been an option. She had really thought she was saving herself by seeking that simple life she'd always dreamed of.

It hadn't worked. Leander had been there, imbuing every inch of beach and rocky hill and placid cove with memories of their honeymoon. And when she had tried to find solace in that whimsical connection to her mother's memory, she had only confronted more of Midas's treachery.

Hatred had nearly consumed her, then. In those moments, she had understood why Leander was so bent on destroying Midas. It had felt as though Midas had ruined *them* and she had wanted to make him pay for all she had lost.

If Midas did tear them apart, however, it would be because she had let it happen. Whether Leander loved her back wasn't important. Leander had helped her believe that she mattered. He had taught her to have courage and strength and had shown her how to stand up for herself. For that, he deserved her love. She would *always* love him.

And in loving him, she held a force more powerful than destructive hate. Love infused her with hope. Love *healed*. Love made her brave enough to pull the things she loved from the fire. And that's where Leander was right now. He was burning up in the flames of hate.

She wanted to lift him out, but would he see it that way?

"They're voting for you. Aren't they?" He was putting it together very quickly. "That's why you brought in a new CEO at Callas."

She held her breath, waiting for the lash of betrayal to strike behind his eyes.

"I was hoping you would support me, too." Her voice was a near whisper. "Justice will be served, Leander. I'll go back as far as I need to ensure it." She clenched her fist on his sleeve. "You don't have to keep fighting to take what you think should be yours." She couldn't interpret what he was thinking as emotions shifted like storm clouds in his gray eyes. "You can put down your weapons and let me give it to you. If you'll trust me to do it?"

Her own eyes were growing damp with distress. He seemed to be growing bigger before her, swelling with something...

Pride? Wonder?

A hot lump of emotion, of optimism, formed behind her breastbone.

"I would trust you with my life, Ilona. With my future. My children. My heart." His warm hand cupped the side of her neck. His smile grew with the fullness that was expanding in her chest. "Of course, I trust you to make things right for me. You already do."

She blinked fast, trying to see him through

her gathering tears, smile wobbling all over the place.

Midas swore disparagingly, saying, "Get a room."

Leander sighed with annoyance. "I move that Midas be removed from his position as president and Ilona appointed in his place effective immediately."

"Second," Hercules said promptly.

Every hand went up except Midas's.

"Motion carried," Hercules noted to the meeting secretary. "I also move that any profit going to Midas from Pagonis International be held in trust pending an investigation into the technology in question. Those funds will be paid to Leander as part of his settlement if wrongdoing is found. It will be," Hercules said with distaste. "Mama left the safe open after collecting her jewelry. I turned over some very interesting documents to Leander's lawyer that our father had kept from that time."

"Second," someone else murmured.

Midas grew more agitated as votes returned a unanimous affirmative.

"You can't *do* this," he insisted.

"Notify Security to escort him out," Leander said to Androu.

"You'll be sorry," Midas said to Ilona as he thrust himself to his feet. "I'll make you pay for this."

"You're making threats in front of witnesses," Leander pointed out and tried to place himself protectively between Midas and her, but Ilona leaned forward against the table, staring down the man she had once feared. He seemed utterly pathetic now. Weak and small.

"Your threat will go in the *minutes*," she told him. "And I'll add it to the evidence of your assault. I advise you to retain good counsel for the plethora of legal problems you are about to encounter."

As Androu let in a security guard, Ilona flicked her tail of hair behind her shoulder.

"*Your* presence is no longer required," she told Midas. *"Get lost."*

Midas left with a kick of a chair toward a window, leaving a web of cracks where it struck. He jerked his arm from the security guard's attempt to hold on to it, but he left.

The whole room exhaled. Everyone looked

to each other with mixtures of shock and astonishment.

They had done it!

Light-headed with triumph, Ilona tried to gather some semblance of order.

"Has everyone met my husband?" she asked, hand shaking as she indicated him, unable to resist a proprietary sweep of her hand down his silk tie. "Leander will be voting my shares for the foreseeable future. He'll recuse when we negotiate my salary, obviously. Let's finish this as quickly as possible." She wanted him to herself. She wanted to go *home*.

She started to walk around to where Hercules was righting the chair Midas had vacated, but Leander caught her hand to draw her back.

"Do you know how incredible you are?" He stood her right in front of him and looked deep into her eyes, not seeming to care they had all these witnesses. "Do you understand how much I admire and love you? Because I love you more than I can express. *Nothing* matters if you're not in my life."

She had to swallow her heart back into place. His words shook her to her core. She was hardly able to bear the naked emotion in his eyes. He could have turned on her, but he loved her. She felt it soaking into her cells and membranes and soul. She might burst with the sheer volume of the seemingly endless pouring of joy into her being.

"I love you, too," she assured him shakily.

His arm looped behind her back and he lightly crushed her into his front.

As his mouth settled on hers, she heard Hercules say with amusement, "That goes in the minutes, too, that they love each other. In case there's any doubt in future."

There wouldn't be.

EPILOGUE

London, two years later...

"SHE'LL BE FINE," Leander's mother assured Ilona. "The nanny is here. We'll have a little play time, a bath, a story and a song... She'll wake in the morning and not even know you weren't here until you're back."

"*I'll* notice," Ilona said plaintively.

Leander didn't admit it, but he suffered hints of separation anxiety, too. It was hard enough to leave Delphine, named for Ilona's mother, for a few hours when they went to work. Leaving her overnight, even with his mother, was a big step.

It was also something Ilona had told him a dozen times was necessary for him to repair his relationship with his mother. *It's a sign of your forgiveness. She needs to know you trust her. She needs a chance to bond with Delphine, too. This is good for all of us.*

He had succumbed to her logic and, truth be told, was already fantasizing about having his wife to himself for a night in a very private and well-appointed hotel room.

First, they had to visit a gallery that was showing Hercules's latest works, though.

"The car is waiting," he reminded her. "We'll leave extra security here if that will make you feel better."

They didn't need security the way they used to. Midas had used his last resources to flee to his mother's New York apartment. He was awaiting extradition to face charges in Athens. He also had various accusations working through courts in a number of other countries, many having come to light as his power to intimidate and retaliate had waned. He would always be a small concern, but Midas had become something unpleasant they only thought about so they could be sure they caught it early, like prostate cancer.

Ilona stole one more pet of Delphine's fine black hair and kissed her little wrinkle-nosed smile and they were away.

"Finally, I have you to myself." He picked up Ilona's hand and kissed her knuckles, noting the coiled ivy climbing toward the knuckle of her index finger. "What's this? Going somewhere?"

"No. I have two things I've been meaning to tell you. First, we have to work out a stretch of time where we can give up both Feodor and Androu."

"Feodor finally proposed?"

"He did." She cocked her head and made a face of sweet sentiment.

"Good for them. Tell them to book whatever works. Androu will figure out how to keep us from imploding in their absence. What else?" He gave the ring a small twist.

"Oh. Um. I thought you'd want to know that I, um…" She glanced at the closed privacy screen and whispered, "I had the doctor remove my IUD."

"You thought you would forget to tell me that?" he asked with amusement and another emotion that was bright and warm. He loved Delphine. Loved her to the moon and back. He and Ilona had talked about more children and he had made it clear he would have a dozen if Ilona was up for it, but he'd left it to her to decide when to try again.

"Sometimes we get carried away." She rolled

her shoulder. "I thought you should be fully informed."

"We do get carried away," he acknowledged, tugging her into leaning close enough he could nibble at the edge of her jaw. "Let's get carried away right now. We don't *really* have to see Hercules, do we?"

"I want to make an appearance so there aren't any hard feelings. Don't," she quickly added, holding up her finger between them. "I heard it as I said it."

A hard feeling was definitely liable to happen. He grinned and snapped his teeth at her finger, so enamored, he was stupid with it. And yes, he was impatient to get her alone, but anticipation had its attractions.

"Do you remember, a long time ago, that you told me the best revenge is to be happy?" he reminded her. "I didn't know I could *be* this happy until you came into my life." Until he had put down his anger and hatred and all the baggage he had carried, and allowed her love to surround him and fill him with this unrelenting contentment. "I'm smug as hell these days."

She blinked and bit a lip that had begun to

tremble with emotion. "We're a good pair then, because I'm completely insufferable, too."

"I'm doing it right?" He touched his thumb to the dampness in the corner of her eye. "Loving you?"

"You really are." She offered her mouth for a soft, lingering kiss that could have turned into more. He couldn't help trailing his fingertips along her bare shoulder and she sighed a small encouragement as he did, but the car halted outside the gallery.

Ilona drew back and moved her ring to her thumb.

"That's to remind me we're only staying a few minutes. We have somewhere important to be. Bed," she mouthed, as if he wasn't already on that page with her.

He helped her from the car, so pleased he was obnoxious with it.

* * * * *

LET'S TALK

Romance

For exclusive extracts, competitions
and special offers, find us online:

f facebook.com/millsandboon

⬚ @millsandboonuk

🐦 @millsandboon

Or get in touch on 0844 844 1351*

For all the latest titles coming soon,
visit millsandboon.co.uk/nextmonth

*Calls cost 7p per minute plus your phone company's price per
minute access charge